Blood Avenger *is a first-rate thriller, a larger-than-life Texas tale of politics, drugs and power that starts quickly and builds to a thundering conclusion.*

Robert Wynne
Former Screenwriter,
"Walker, Texas Ranger"

BLOOD AVENGER

BLOOD AVENGER

by
Julian Stuart Haber

LONGHORN CREEK PRESS

First Edition
Printed and bound in the United States of America

ISBN 0-9714358-8-X
Library of Congress Control Number 2005920242

Inquiries for volume purchases of this book may be directed to
Wilson & Associates
101 South Johnson
Alvin, Texas 77511
www.thebookdistributor.com

For personalized, autographed copies, contact
Sales@LonghornCreekPress.com or by mail to
Longhorn Creek Press, Sales Department
2438 10th Street
Irving, Texas 75060

Please visit www.LonghornCreekPress.com
and www.bloodavenger.com

Dedication

In memory of my cousin

Sondra

*Hope, faith, and meditation
can help soften any pain.*

Acknowledgments

The author wishes to recognize Deputy Sam Haber, Officer Jon Haber, Fire Marshal paramedic Howard Haber, and Dr. Lawrence Haber for technical advice concerning police, court, legal, and medical examiner procedures. Mary Dobbins contributed suggestions relative to various aspects of religious material.

I wish to also thank the DFW Writers' Workshop for hours of listening to the text and offering critique. Ron and Caryl McAdoo from that group were particularly helpful, as was our Saturday sub-group Linda, Constance, Tom, and Marybear.

My friend Camille Cline, my editor for one of my previously published non-fiction books, offered significant editorial comment.

Lastly, my wife, Marian, who helped with revision after revision, put up with reams of discarded paper, and whose love continued to support me during this entire project.

SO THAT THE BLOOD
OF THE INNOCENT
NOT BE SHED

DEUTERONOMY 19:10

1 The Accident

I sat at my mother's side and held her frail hand. Bones protruded through her yellowed skin. The room smelled like decaying meat left too long out of the refrigerator.

Through her shallow labored breaths, she tried to whisper, but most of the time, the words neither formed on her lips nor made any sense. The cancer had spread everywhere, and now, I just waited. Waited for G-d to be merciful and end it.

She groaned every few seconds, her face contorted with pain. A nurse injected a dose of morphine, and soon, peace descended upon her. Her level of consciousness then increased. After a time, she squeezed my hand. "You must not let them live. You know who they are."

I partially closed my eyes, and a lump swelled in my throat. "What are you talking about, Momma?"

"Those boys killed him." She paused and breathed

deeply as if to brace against the pain of the past and present.

"That was a long time ago. They really did nothing wrong." I brushed back a stray wisp of white hair from her brow. "We don't know who was responsible."

"But they put him in that position!" She coughed from exhaustion. "If not for them, he'd be alive and here with me. You and he—the only good things—the only good things I had. Those boys took him away forever."

"I know that, but, Momma, it was an accident."

She groaned again, and her dark sunken eyes held mine with a renewed strength. "You must promise. You must promise me, or I will make sure G-d puts a curse on you." The strength faded faster than it came. For a second her eyes begged, then she whispered. "Take care of them. They killed him—no one was punished. The police did nothing. The university did nothing. No one did anything. Promise me so I can die in peace."

She lapsed into a deep sleep and alternatively stopped breathing for a few seconds and then pulled air in with what little strength was left in her.

I shook my head. What a hateful and absurd request.

I left my mother's side for a few minutes. Sorrow ground my nerves. Her hatred served only to make my already down mood worse. Thank goodness for Prozac. Without it, I might have broken completely.

Suddenly, her breathing became even more labored. She reached. I stepped to her side. She pulled me against her thinning breasts. "Promise me, son," she whispered.

My tears moistened her nightgown. "Okay, Mom. Okay. Die in peace. I'll take care of everything."

She paled, her lips blued, and she no longer breathed. I could have called the hospital staff to resuscitate her, but why bother? I just sat there with my mouth tightly pursed and rested my sadness and pain. I placed my aching head into my hands.

After a while I regained my composure, kissed her on the cheek, and pulled the sheet over her face.

*　*　*　*　*

Austin, 1970

"Don't remove the blindfold until you count to one hundred and fifty. Understand, Pledge?" The sergeant-of-arms shoved Aaron. He tripped over tree roots and fell to the sloping ground.

"Y-y-yes, sir." Aaron patted the ground up to the trunk, then turned and scooted on his butt until he pressed his back against the huge old tree. The tightly knotted fabric over his eyes seemed like a vise squeezing his pounding head.

He counted aloud. "One-two-three-four-five..."

The forest resounded with owl hoots and the electronic click of insects. A coyote wailed off in the distance. Gusting through the hills, a north wind stirred the trees and rattled leaves and branches. A car's tires screeched and threw gravel pulling away. Nature's symphony chilled his blood and exaggerated his aloneness, but he didn't move. Not yet.

"...sixty-three, sixty-four, sixty-five, sixty-six. This stinks. He ripped off the blindfold to an impenetrable darkness.

At least he knew which way was down. Maybe he should wait until morning. The sun would come up in a few hours, and in the daylight he'd have no trouble finding his way. With the tree at his back, he held his knees and shivered.

An eerie pair of illuminated eyes stared from the woods. They surveyed him, gave him the creeps. Then something fell from the enormous tree and slapped his shoulder. A thick snake slithered across his arm, and he froze. It crossed his torso and reached his legs. Aaron didn't even take a breath. Brushing over his bare feet, the reptile's thrusting tongue flicked his skin.

Once his eyes finally adapted to the darkness, he watched it move back a few inches into a coil ready to strike. It rattled, its head suspended in the air. Aaron swallowed. It slithered beyond his feet.

Sweat soaked him like a heavy rain. His heart pounded and lost all sense of rhythm and order. He took several deep breaths. He would survive only if he left this place. Left it now.

He fanned the air and brushed the trunk of a younger tree. He grabbed ahold and scooted downward, patting the air with his free hand. He could hold onto the trees and work his way down the mountain. Forget waiting for daylight. Anything was better than staying up there.

He used caution, placing one foot barely in front of

the other. Branch by branch, tree by tree, he baby-stepped his way down. After what seemed like hours, he finally came upon a narrow road.

Off in the distance a bit above him, headlights shone brightly in the black night. It would be great to beat those frat boys to the house. He ran toward the car on the smooth surface.

*   *   *   *   *

First-term state legislator Bentsen Russell drove in a trance. Time spent with his attractive blue-eyed assistant always affected him this way. Quite often, they'd meet in his small rental cottage concealed in the hills just north of Austin. A couple of drinks and energetic sex wearied him. His mind drifted.

What a good time. Extra special, he mused, and just forty-five minutes back to Austin. He patted the dashboard in search of a pack of cigarettes.

He clicked his bright beams to cut the darkness and sped through the night. Around a sudden curve, he fought for control of his red Pontiac Grand Prix. Tires screeched on the cool asphalt. His heart pounded.

He reduced his speed to fifty and rolled down the windows, hoping the brisk morning air would revive him. However, he still battled to keep his eyes open. He hugged another corner into a twisting S-turn surrounded by boulders.

His headlights illuminated something ahead on the

road. What was it? He hit his brakes hard, but the Grand Prix lost traction and went into a skid. A sickening thud echoed through his soul. Was it a deer?

It smashed against the headlights, flipped up and shattered the windshield. The body rolled backwards and to the side. Flesh and metal grated against the boulders. The car came to a jarring stop. Russell shouldered his door and vomited.

His muscles ached. His neck stiffened, and his head throbbed where it struck the steering wheel. He set the emergency brake and stumbled out of the car.

He approached the animal with caution. The carcass lay still smashed against the side of the hill.

Oh, dear G-d.

It was a person. A young man.

What was he doing out on this lonely stretch of road in the middle of the night? Jagged bones extruded through torn flesh. Russell placed his head to the youth's chest and listened.

Nothing.

He pressed his fingers on the side of the boy's neck. No pulse. He shook his head. How could this be? Tears rolled down his cheek. What was the kid thinking, wearing a dark shirt and blue jeans?

Russell examined the morbid scene. He needed to clear his mind. His opponent had narrowed the gap between them to four percentage points. He wiped his sweaty palms on his shirt. His belly growled, and a knot formed in his throat.

2 Blackmail

A faint glow crept over the top of the hills announcing the impeding arrival of the sun. He sobbed. How could this happen? He looked up the road, from where he came. Someone might come along at any time.

He wanted to call the police and an ambulance, but he hesitated. The kid was already dead anyway. If it hit the news, they'd crucify him. He jumped back into the car and sped to his family's ranch thirty miles away.

Once there, he opened the rear gate and drove down the dirt road about a half mile, then across the pasture to the largest stock tank on the place. He eased up on the grass covered earthen dam until he reached the middle then yanked the wheels around.

He gunned the motor. The car lurched forward. He opened the door and jumped. The dark murky water engulfed him. He bobbed to the surface, just in time to see the Pontiac's back bumper slip under water. He shivered.

The sky grew brighter. He trudged onto the bank hugging himself. A few hundred yards away, an empty shed offered shelter from the cool morning air. Inside, he rummaged until he found jeans, a shirt and boots. What a stroke of luck that he had stashed them there last summer when he helped the ranch hands repair fence posts.

He grabbed a shovel, dug a shallow hole behind the shed, and buried his wet clothing and boots. Then he covered his dig with leaves and branches. He jogged up to the house, commandeered a ranch pickup and drove it home to Austin.

By ten-thirty, Russell had entered his campaign head-quarters on Fifteenth Street in downtown Austin. Volunteers ran in and out collecting signs to post and pamphlets to distribute. A patriotic blur of red, white, and blue covered the walls.

Prim and proper in a stylish gray business suit with a paisley maroon scarf, Alice, his assistant, sat at a small desk in the middle of the room commanding a small cohort of workers folding mail.

She playfully batted her baby blues. "Y'all sleep well? You look kinda beat."

"Depends on what you call sleep, darlin'."

After greeting several others, he sat at his desk. A large envelope sealed with postal tape and unstamped from the Guadalajara Tourist bureau beckoned.

To The Honorable Bentsen Russell
Personal / For Your Eyes Only

He opened it, pulled out a colored photograph of the Las Cabañas Church and Orphanage and an accompanying letter.

Dear Sir,

The Las Cabañas orphanage has served homeless and poor children of Guadalajara for more than a century. We are drastically in need of funds to help continue our good deeds. We know you are from a charitable family and suggest you make a $50,000 donation. The check should be made to Save The Poor Children Foundation and mailed to the Central Cayman Bank, 1002 Empire Street, Grand Cayman, Cayman Islands. Your prompt attention to this matter will work in your favor. A note awaits you behind a loose stone in front of your cottage.

Sincerely,
Father Diablo

Russell felt the color drain from his face. His knees weakened. He really didn't want to go back to the rental house. Memory of the previous evening's events reverberated in his head like a relentless banging hammer. But, as if driven by a demon, he tried to stand and walk.

He faltered and grabbed a chair and the corner of his

desk. Where had up gone?

He caught a glimpse of Alice and righted himself. He gestured to her. She came closer, but he continued his retreat toward the door.

"What's happened to you?"

"Something's come up. Be back in a couple of hours. Can you cover things?"

Without waiting for her reply, he left and drove the old ranch pickup truck toward his love cottage in the hills. Sweat dripped from his brow, and his foot pushed the gas pedal three quarters of the way down. Who had seen what? Was this about his affair or had someone seen the accident?

A wailing siren pierced his ear. He checked the speedometer and mentally cursed. Blinking red, white, and blue lights danced in his rear view mirror. He couldn't believe his luck. Russell told himself to remain calm as he pulled to the side of the road. He lowered his window and started digging for his wallet.

A short muscular officer in a crisp blue uniform appeared. "Did you realize you were going sixty in a residential zone? License, please."

Russell examined his accuser. "Terribly, sorry. I'm a state Senator and was on the way to an important meeting. Guess my mind drifted."

Pulling a booklet from his pocket, the officer began to write. Russell looked at the policeman's nameplate. "Officer Anderson?"

"Yes, sir."

He glared at the policeman. "You must be new. Representatives usually have immunity in the capital."

Scratching his head, Anderson continued to calmly write the ticket. "May be a rookie, but I'm not stupid. In my book, legislators should be held to a higher standard than others. It's a mighty poor example doing sixty in a neighborhood. You could kill somebody that way, you know."

"What's your badge number? Your disrespect and ill behavior will be reported to your superiors."

The young officer looked straight into Russell's eyes. "The name is Anderson, John Anderson, shield eight-four-six-nine-one. Go right ahead and report me, sir." He handed over the ticket. "Have a good day, Mr. Russell."

"Yeah right." He semi-accidentally squealed the pick-up's tires and headed north into the hills. He watched his speed, but was there in no time.

Swaying in a strong north wind, oak and pecan trees cast intermittent shadows against the cottage's old brown carved stones. Sun rays peeked from behind the rapidly moving clouds.

Russell ran to the door, and wiggled the adjacent stones. They all felt firm in perfect position, some round, some octagonal, but all snug.

One by one he checked for a loose stone. At the bottom left side, a small stone moved at his touch. He worked it free with the help of his pocketknife. Reaching into the cavity, he felt a piece of damp, folded paper and opened it.

> *THOU SHALT NOT COMMIT ADULTERY.*
> *THOU SHALL BE THY BROTHER'S KEEPER.*
> *THOU SHALT NOT MURDER.*
> *ONLY CHARITY WILL AVERT THE SEVERE*
> *DECREE.*
> *WE SAW YOU.*
> *FOLLOW OUR INSTRUCTIONS PRECISELY OR*
> *WE WILL TELL ALL.*
> *FATHER DIABLO*

*   *   *   *   *

At four o'clock in the afternoon, officers Carl Phillips of the Austin PD and Alvin Myers from the University of Texas police department rang Kappa Gamma's house bell. The two assembled the frat brothers in the living room.

Myers studied the faces of those present. "We regret to inform you that Aaron Michaels was killed by a hit-and-run driver near Mount Bonnell earlier today."

A murmur of whispers filled the room followed by an occasional, "Oh no."

"Who's in charge?"

"I'm Arnold Weiss, fraternity president. This is awful news, officer."

"We know Kappa Gamma's hazing practices, boys. Is

that why the Michaels kid was on the road?"

"N-n-no sir."

Myers grabbed the boy by the shoulders and squeezed him with an iron grip until his skin began to blanch. "Look, we were here last year when the kid from Mexico tried to kill himself and you gave us a real hard time. If you stall us now, we'll run the lot of you in and recommend the university president close down this house."

"Okay, okay." The kid pulled away. "What do you want us to do?"

3 Old Brothers

Rain soaked my face and dripped off my hat as I knelt by her grave. "Momma, my heart aches. I know I'm disappointing you, but I just can't hurt those boys. Just isn't right no matter how I play it in my mind."

The rain turned into small pellets of ice and then into quarter-sized hail that stung my skin and bounced off my raincoat. Bright red spots and whelps rose on my hands and face. They ached and itched something awful, but no matter how much I scratched, the pain wouldn't go away.

"Momma, don't be angry. The Bible says to love thy neighbor as thyself, not to hurt him. Now, how can I go against the scriptures?" I tried to ease my pain and leaned against her tombstone for strength.

"Don't be mad at me. For G-d's sake don't be mad at

me." I wiped my nose and sniffled.

Thunder resounded through the air. One forceful, unbearable roar after another burst through me. Lightning flashed across the heavens, illuminating the dreary sky. Shuddering, I cupped my hands and buried my face in them.

"How I wish I could change places with you. It must be easier to rest in the ground than be sitting here grieving. I've tried to make you proud. Lots of money, I'm a real success, mind you. Much more than anyone else in the family before me ever achieved.

"I established a charity in your name. We've helped so many churches, orphanages, unfortunate kids, and families. Isn't that enough? To do good and help others. Please, Momma, be proud of me. I'm so frightened. Please release me."

I gazed at the heavens and they became more infuriated. Light and dark clouds commingled, bubbling higher into the atmosphere. The wind howled and moved them into gray swirling circles that took aim at the ground below.

"Please stop, Momma. I can't do it. I can't kill them. *THOU SHALT NOT MURDER*," I screamed.

The enraged sky answered with a powerful lightning bolt that slammed into a tree right behind me. The old oak's trunk split all the way to the roots. It smoldered with fire and smoke. Then one half of the great tree fell toward me in slow motion across my mother's grave and came to rest inches from my skull.

I knew then, I must fulfill my promise.

*   *   *   *   *

Austin, 1993

Adam Cain's Rolls Royce raced down the freeway that dissected the five massive concrete and steel semi-circular terminals of DFW International Airport. At the curb of terminal Three E, his chauffeur opened the rear door. "This should put you right in front of gate 22, Mr. Cain."

"Thank you." Adam straightened the jacket of his two-thousand dollar tailored English suit, reveled in his expensive Italian shoes and put on an air of polite arrogance. He loved flaunting his wealth and power. He walked with a deliberate stride to the gate and arrived in time to hear the passenger agent's announcement.

"Flight 453 to Austin will begin boarding. At this time first class, gold, and platinum passengers only, please."

Adam moved to the end of the line. He placed his hands in his pockets and rubbed two quarters together. He loosened his tie and unbuttoned his collar. Why wait? He fished out a five-milligram Valium, snapped it in two then swallowed each half dry. When in control of his own aircraft, he had no fear of flying, but he hated boarding commercial flights, putting his life in another pilot's hands. Bad timing, his Gulfstream being in for repairs.

Twenty minutes after he took his seat, the plane taxied down the tarmac to the runway. Soon, it raced forward and moved upward at an acute angle to the ground until there was only sky ahead and a miniature landscape below. He dozed off almost immediately. It seemed he barely closed his eyes when the intercom blared and interrupted his sleep.

"Captain here. We're about fifteen minutes out of Austin, and our in-flight-radar indicates several storm cells in the area. Flight attendants take your landing positions. Everyone remain seated with your seat belts fastened. Sorry, folks, it might get a little rough."

Outside the window, threatening clouds merged and stacked one on top of the other into one great massive black wall. All of a sudden, the sunlight disappeared and darkness engulfed the plane. Lightning played across the sky in the distance.

He hated being level with the bolts of free-flowing electrical impulses. It scared him to death.

Pellets of rain and sleet pounded the aircraft's windows and body. Adam clung to his armrests and pressed his back farther into the plush seat. He manipulated the handles and moved his feet against the footrest as if he were flying and in control.

He sure wouldn't try to land in this maelstrom. Much better to fly above the clouds awhile and then slip around them.

The plane fell faster and faster. It seemed beyond the safe rate of descent. Felt like the craft was about to be slammed into the ground by the hand of G-d.

The engines whined and struggled. At first, louder with more power as though compensating for severe downdrafts. Then they ominously cut back to near silence, adjusting for sudden updrafts. A strong burst of power forced the plane upward until it cleared the cloud wall. Sunshine glistened off its wet brushed aluminum.

"Captain again. Sorry about that, but looks like we're out of it." Thirty minutes later, the pilot set her down at Robert Muller Airport.

Although Adam traveled to the capital many times each month to conduct business and lobby the legislature, this trip marked a very special occasion. His good friend and college roommate, Travis Hamilton III, had invited him to attend the announcement of his candidacy for governor of the State of Texas. Not only a great opportunity for contacts, but the exposure Adam relished.

As a student at the University of Texas, Hamilton had passed undergraduate and law school by the most narrow of margins. However, he married into a wealthy and influential Austin family. With their financial backing and connections, he won his way into the Texas State House of Representatives.

During his second term in office, a group of fellow legislators approached him and asked his help in passing laws favorable to the Mexican Mafia, but he immediately contacted the authorities. One of Austin's finest, a detective by the name of John Anderson, wired

Hamilton up and exposed the entire scheme. He rode the coattails of that case right into the Texas Senate.

Adam snickered. While heroes didn't always make the best public officials, they almost always got themselves elected. Still, it would be good to see his friend again.

Once off the aircraft, his anxiety dissipated. Adam exited the jet-bridge to the terminal where the first thing he noticed was a striking brunette with soft hazel eyes who held a small cardboard sign. The milling crowd threatened to distract him, but his eyes remained fixed on the exquisite woman.

He moved closer and glanced at the card. Things were looking up. Printed in large bold letters: "**CAIN**."

He caught her glance, and the gaze hung suspended in space in a brief, animated moment of excitement. "I'm Adam Cain."

"Good morning. I'm Monica Gutierrez, Senator Hamilton's senior legislative aide. He asked me to welcome you to Austin. Any luggage?"

He hesitated, almost embarrassed, as his eyes traced her sculptured figure. "Uh, no." Adam cleared his throat. "I travel light." He pointed to a small carry-on.

"Excellent. Then we're ready to go."

He followed her to a black Continental in the short-term lot. In the distance, the storm that impeded 453's descent moved off to the south. The sun sparkled, and the air smelled fresh and clean.

She clicked the automatic lock. The plush gray seats

and new car scent comforted Adam like it always did.

Leaving the airport, the Lincoln soon reached the interstate that ran alongside the city, past the Johnson Library, the University of Texas, and the grandiose pink Capitol surrounded by an ocean of pristine white state office buildings.

At the bridge crossing Town Lake, a wide-dammed area of the lower Colorado River that divided Austin, Monica finally spoke. "Senator Hamilton has a condo on the lake. He thought it would be nice if you stayed in the same building, so he arranged the use of a friend's unit."

"Sounds good. Should beat staying at a hotel."

He liked the sound of her voice, and her smile amazed him. "How long have you worked for Travis?"

She smiled again. "I started as an intern in my senior year at UT then stayed on after graduation. That was nearly six years ago. I understand you knew him when you were both students at the university."

"Yeah. About twenty-five years now." Adam loosened his seatbelt. "Where you from?"

"Edinburg, in the valley."

Adam nodded. He placed his lower lip between his teeth and pulled it back against them. "What's our schedule like?"

"Pretty hectic once we get going." She turned onto Riverside Drive. "But you have a couple of hours to relax and freshen up. I'll escort you to the hotel where the Senator will announce his candidacy."

"Will I have a chance to talk to him?"

"Oh, sure. He's just one floor above you. I imagine he'll come down as soon as he's heard you've arrived."

After a few blocks, she turned into a driveway lined on both sides with well-landscaped gardens. A handsome twelve-story brick building loomed ahead. He followed her into the building's glass-lined elevator and studied the graceful curves. Her warm hazel eyes and radiant face sent a tingle through him.

No matter how hard he tried, he couldn't deter his little boy smile.

On the fourth floor, she exited and led him down the hall. "Here we are. Four-o-seven." She unlocked then opened the door. Beautiful French provincial furniture graced the well-appointed condo. A view of Town Lake, wall tapestries and elegant paintings and two fireplaces completed the ambience.

He walked a short distance to the outdoor terrace. A small flotilla of sailboats drifted on the lake. "Nice view, isn't it?" All of a sudden, a speedboat slashed through the little regatta, leaving a huge wake that capsized several boats.

A gush of anger heated his face, and his gut burned. "Did you see that? Those miserable speedboat freaks never even came back to help."

She took his hand in hers and held it for a fleeting second before giving a little squeeze. "Yes, I sure did. How rude, but it doesn't look like anyone was hurt."

He stowed his anger and forced himself to a state of calm. "Can you — stay a little longer?"

"Wish I could." She raised her eyebrows and smiled. "Have to get all dressed up for tonight. I'm not far, though, one floor below you. Besides, the Senator should be down to visit in a little while. I'll be back in an hour and a half or so."

After she left, Adam inspected the condo. He had two large bedrooms, both with mirrored ceilings and round queen-sized beds, to choose from. He dropped his carry-on in the first. Brick embellished with white marble encased the fireplaces in it and the living room, and a slate base added a nice touch.

Hmm, a well-stocked wet bar. The dining area was modest, but it appeared the kitchen had been recently modernized. The fresh scent of pine oil and lemon wafted in the air.

The doorbell chimed "*The Eyes of Texas are Upon You.*" Adam sauntered to the foyer, set the door ajar with the chain still in place, and peered into the corridor. Two big, muscular guys stared back, but the imposing six-foot-seven frame of his friend dwarfed them both.

Travis' craggy masculine face with an angled jaw and his trim build hadn't changed. His old buddy shrugged and held a hand palm up. "You gonna let us in or what? I've got a speech to give in a couple of hours."

Adam fumbled with the chain and opened the door. The senator embraced him before they touched thumbs, rubbed their palms together, then clasped hands to form a V at the wrists. It all came back without a thought. Funny what the brain retains.

"So, how are things in big D?"

"Can't complain. Business is great. But how about you? I am so proud of you. Who would have ever thought it? You, governor." He pointed to the two men. "And who might these gentlemen be?"

"Meet Al Gonzales and Tommy Joe Smith, my bodyguards."

"You guys never leave Senator Hamilton's side?"

"No, sir." The taller and darker one extended his hand.

Travis' forehead furrowed, and he looked at the ceiling. "At least not these days. Catching bad guys doesn't always make you friends in this town. One can never be too safe."

"You ever hear what happened to any of our old college gang? I never hear from any of them." Adam strolled toward the bar.

"Got a campaign donation a couple of years ago from Anthony Carr. He lives in Hong Kong now. Made his fortune in the import/export business."

Adam smiled and shook his head in bewilderment. "Who would of thunk it? He was such a geeky twerp. Remember the time that hotshot pre-law student tried to run you out of the frat? That guy's a big time lawyer up my way. What was his name? Jack—? "

"Oh, yeah, the Freed kid." He smiled. "We reconciled after he convinced me he knew every good-looking chick on campus." He paused and looked out over the lake. "Adam, you know I'm favored in the polls. They say I'm a shoo-in, but that's bull. The opera ain't over until the fat lady's sung.

"You're successful and respected in the Metroplex, plus you got a good feel for the economic environment, trends and people. I need someone who can keep me tuned into the business sector and raise funds as the campaign progresses. After I'm elected, I'll need an advisor I can trust. I'd like to count on you."

Adam poured scotch over rocks. "I presume this is what you still drink." He handed it to his friend. "You're one of the few honest politicians I know. I'd be honored."

Hamilton accepted the drink with one hand, gulped it down and raised the other in triumph. "All right. That's great." He looked at his watch. "Well, better go. We'll talk more tonight. Monica's picking you up."

"Right. And if I may say, you have excellent taste." The two men exchanged the Kappa Gamma handshake and the senator departed almost as rapidly as he had arrived. His bodyguards followed close behind.

4 The Declaration

An hour later, Monica knocked. A green sequined dress wrapped her snugly and accentuated her curvaceous figure. Diamonds and emeralds encircled her neck, and she wore matching teardrop earrings that brought out her soft hazel eyes.

He followed her into the mirror-lined elevator. She touched him shoulder to thigh for a moment as the doors closed. His skin warmed and his heart fluttered. Out front, three identical, highly polished Lincoln limousines with whitewall tires lined the semicircular driveway.

"What's going on?" Adam raised his eyebrows.

"It creates a protective environment. The senator's in the first car. Guests always ride in the third. The middle one has a driver and a couple of mannequins. It acts as a decoy." She winked.

He shook his head at the absolute paranoia. The

convoy drove to the Renaissance Hotel in north Austin by way of the Capitol of Texas Highway. Bathed in red, white, and blue spotlights, the grandiose nine-story hotel towered ahead.

When Adam first stayed at the Renaissance some years ago, the scenic views of the lush green and flowered hills surrounding Austin lured guests. Although a small forest and beautiful gardens remained behind the hotel, time and progress had not been kind to the vistas, replacing the once magnificent scenery with tall office buildings and shopping centers.

A huge flag sporting the lone star waved beside the Stars and Stripes from above the overhang that covered the entrance.

Monica took Adam's arm as he passed through a small lobby into a large atrium that rose to the very top of the building. Landscaped balconies embellished with beautiful plants, statues, and banners wrapped the atrium's interior.

Resounding trumpets, obviously from the University of Texas band, blared "Texas, Our Texas" which echoed in the cavernous space. Hanging from the higher floors, signs and posters declared: "**Travis Hamilton III, Next Governor of Texas.**" Drifting at various heights, hundreds of red, white, and blue balloons filled the air.

Adam scanned all the way to the top noting several glass elevators, reception rooms, and a marble staircase that led downstairs. If his friend was so paranoid about an assassination attempt, then why would he book such a place?

A protocol officer assembled the entourage for a grand entry into the main ballroom. Travis entered first with U.S. Secretary of State Russell at his side. Russell, the former U.S. senator from Texas for sixteen years, led the charge. Many considered him the dean of Travis' party.

The staffer positioned Texas State Treasurer Lucille Robbins on Travis' left. Next in the procession, Judge Nathan Coleman of the Texas State Court of Criminal appeals, the first African-American to be elected to statewide office, followed by State Senator Guadalupe Hernandez from Corpus Christi.

Behind the dignitaries came Adam with Monica on his arm, a few other personal friends, a series of political aides, and the security people. One of Travis' personal bodyguards, Al, fronted the procession, and the other, Tommy Joe, covered the rear.

An army of photographers, media personnel, and television cameramen gathered behind ribboned stanchions vying for Hamilton's attention. He was ushered through the gauntlet into the ballroom for his announcement. Security guards struggled to keep pace with Travis, who grasped every hand thrust toward him.

He patted new and old cronies' backs. Much to the obvious frustration of his private guards, every now and then, he fell out of line and into the roaring crowd.

Jan Stern, Travis' press secretary, gave him a firm nudge in the ribs, but spoke just loudly enough to be heard by those close by. "Come on, senator, we have a schedule to keep. Want to miss the early evening news?"

More red, white, and blue canopied the front stage several feet above the main floor. A large map of Texas and a lone star flag adorned the podium. Another band played patriotic music at a considerably softer volume than the glaring brass of the entry orchestra.

An entirely new bevy of television cameras and press had situated themselves in strategic positions near the front of the podium. The white-hot glare of hundreds of mini-suns bathed the speaker's platform. Adam's spirits soared with the exaltation of the moment.

All of a sudden, the chanting began. A few well-placed cheerleaders started the process, screaming over and over again in a harmonious rhythm, "Ham-il-ton, Ham-il-ton." The few voices grew into a thunderous chorus.

"We want Travis, we want Travis," another group began, and the new refrain soon vibrated throughout the hall. The supposed spontaneous demonstration lasted exactly fifteen minutes.

Senator Hernandez, a short woman with coarse features and jet-black hair, rose from her chair on the platform and walked past Secretary Russell, Adam, Monica and the other dignitaries at a slow pace until she reached the speaker's stand.

She gazed out as the crowd continued the rhythmic cheering. Smiling, she cast both arms fully extended above her head, her large palms facing forward, signaling the faithful to quiet down. The clamor continued for a few seconds longer.

"Time to get the show on the road." She motioned down one more time. The cheering again rang out and then died off in gradual declining pulses, until a hushed silence settled.

"Ladies and gentlemen, señores and señoras, it is my great privilege to introduce my good friend, the former senior senator for the great state of Texas, the Secretary of State of the United States of America, and wisest of all public servants who ever represented us, The Honorable Bentsen Russell."

The band played with greater intensity, rocking the room, and the partisan crowd burst into near frenzied applause.

Adam moved his rump about his seat. Not another introduction. Get the show on the road. Get to Travis.

Secretary Russell, a handsome gentleman with snowy gray hair that partially draped his furrowed forehead, scanned his audience in a dignified, authoritative manner.

"Okay, okay, let's quiet down." The crowd responded. "Thank you for this marvelous reception, but we all know the real reason everyone came tonight. We're here to hand the mantle of government of our great state to a young and bright Texan from Killeen.

"This man can and will lead Texas into a future with courage, with brilliance, with honesty, and without fear of the nay-sayers and wrongdoers who threaten the fabric of our society.

"Travis Hamilton is no newcomer, ladies and gentlemen. He and I have worked together for many years at various levels of government to benefit all Texans. I knew him first at the University of Texas where he was a leader in student government. I knew him when he served in the lower house where he refused to be bribed and went after those who would corrupt and rob their fellow Texans."

His voice softened. "Travis Hamilton paid dearly for that honesty. I was at his side at that devastating time in his life when his beloved wife Vickie was murdered."

Tears formed in Adam's eyes. He remembered well the day Vickie's convertible plunged into a deep ravine after her brakes were cut. The death had put Travis into a deep depression, and Adam thought for a while that it might make his friend quit politics altogether.

Russell rambled on. His voice picked up in volume and almost shuddered as it rose. "But neither threats, nor personal harm to his family, nor innuendo, nor hatred could stop this man. I was there when Travis won election to the state senate. He has served our people with care, honesty, dignity, and respect."

For a few seconds he paused and gazed at his audience. Then even in a deeper and more profound tone declared, "And I am honored to be here now to introduce to you a man who does not need introduction to this forum. To offer my whole-hearted support for the most qualified individual to declare his intention to run for governor of the great State of Texas."

His voice crescendoed to the point of exuberant shouting. "Fellow Texans, I give you our next governor, Travis Hamilton, the Third."

The ballroom once again erupted in unison. "TRAVIS, TRAVIS, TRAVIS!" The band pounded out "The Eyes of Texas Are Upon You" over and over again, but the chanting crowd almost drowned it out.

Travis finally stepped to the podium. He turned from side to side, waved, and scanned the crowd. "Thank you, thank you." He interrupted the cheers. Soon they reverted to a semblance of quiet.

"And thank you, Secretary Russell. You've been a good friend. I'm glad we could pull you away from your golf game for this little shindig." Travis chuckled and half saluted the secretary. "It gives me great pleasure to announce before so many friends, supporters, and colleagues that I will indeed seek my party's nomination for the office of governor of this great state of Texas."

The audience once again erupted. Brightly colored placards bounced up and down. A large banner dropped from the apex of the ballroom.

TRAVIS HAMILTON III
GOVERNOR OF TEXAS
WITHOUT FEAR
FOR THE PEOPLE

Red, white, and blue balloons printed with a solitary star fell like rain both from a large net in the rear of the room and from the ceiling.

After a brief period, Travis motioned his supporters to cease their revelry. In a deep voice and slow, rhythmic tone, he accented his key points with his fisted hand thrust toward his audience.

Adam leaned back in his seat on the stage. His eyes closed and opened again several times as he fought off drowsiness. His mind drifted as the senator's speech moved to education and more mundane topics.

Travis reached out to the audience with both hands. "Patricia Lovett may give pleasant speeches, but she neither does her homework nor her job. She promised no more unqualified appointees, that her staff would scrupulously examine backgrounds, that there would be no more good-ol'-boys systems.

"But Mrs. Lovett turned around and appointed Laura Hodges, her close personal friend, as head of the Agricultural Commission. Well, we all know what happened with that one. The closest Laura ever came to managing a farm or ranch, let alone a state regulatory agency, was consuming a medium-rare steak and salad at her country club."

A few scattered laughs echoed through the hall.

"Governor Lovett never bothered to verify her friend's education or her background, just appointed her anyway. What a disaster and embarrassment that turned out to be for our state.

"Read my lips. I will appoint only those who are highly qualified. I promise the abolishment of the good-ol'-boys and good-ol'-girls systems for state offices. So, those of you who are the unqualified good-ol'-boys and girls, you might as well get up and leave right now. I am definitely not your man."

A smattering of applause and nervous chatter flowed.

"I promise you that beginning tomorrow morning, I will hit the ground running to secure our party's nomination, win the gubernatorial election, and then fulfill these dreams for all the citizens of our state; men, women, and children alike. All of us together must fan out across the vastness of this great and wondrous state and carry our message to people everywhere."

The ballroom once again erupted into loud cheering. Over and over again the crowd chanted. "We want Hamilton! We want Hamilton!"

Travis raised open hands triumphantly into the air and waved back and forth to his faithful supporters. Adam, Monica, and the other guests and aides joined the politician around the podium. Security opened a large path from the stage, and the entire assemblage emptied out of the ballroom toward the adjoining atrium.

If there were going to be no more good-ol'-boys or girls, one could not tell it this evening. More self-interested individuals and groups schmoozed with each other than could be counted or acknowledged.

Monica briefly introduced Adam to Secretary Russell then moved toward the bar. "His endorsement is a lock on the nomination."

"Then why the circus?"

BLOOD AVENGER

"We have two campaigns events. Tonight and then the big show in a couple of months. Publicity and exposure is what it's all about. You know that."

"But Lovett's still governor. She still represents this party, doesn't she? Why are all the heavyweights throwing their support to someone else?"

Monica shrugged. "Politics are fickle. Depends on many factors."

"Like what?"

"Like a rumor that a big bomb is about to drop on the statehouse. The party will need a hard hitter like Travis to take her place."

Adam frowned. "What's the rumor?"

Her eyes narrowed, and her faced hardened. "I can't discuss it right now. Please don't ask."

"Come on. I'm supposedly a top advisor for this election. I should know whatever's going on." He guided her out of the crowded atrium and slipped into an adjoining meeting room.

"Laura Hodges lives in the statehouse with Lovett much of the time. A tabloid photographer took a picture of them together in a, shall we say compromising position. The party has purchased the photographs, and we're pretty sure there aren't any others, but sooner or later something like that is bound to leak.

"Lovett's toast. She can either quit now or not run for reelection."

Just then, the door to the meeting room swung open. The state treasurer stood in the entryway. She cut a trim figure, her face accentuated by piercing blue eyes. Blond hair fell to her shoulders.

"Monica, who is this handsome devil, and why are you keeping him all for yourself? Y'all need to come out and join the party."

"Lucille, I'd like you to meet Adam Cain, an old friend of Senator Hamilton's and a personal advisor."

"Well, how nice to finally meet you. Travis speaks quite sentimentally of you."

"Uh, oh, that can't be good." He motioned the ladies out to the main reception area, stopped at the bar and handed each a gin and tonic before accepting the third for himself. His encounter with the lovely public servant proved brief as Lucille obviously caught the eye of a prestigious reporter and excused herself.

"Anything between her and Travis?"

"No, they're just good friends, most of the time."

"How about you and Travis?"

Monica giggled. "Come on, Adam. I would never mix business and pleasure. Be like making out with your brother."

"Never?"

"No, never."

"What about me?"

"You're a guest." She winked and playfully eased her elbow into his side.

 # 5 The Morning After

After about three hours, people began to filter out of the hotel. It could have been sooner for Adam.

"Any of you like to join me at my place for a night-cap?" Travis asked.

Secretary Russell shook his head. "Not me. I try to avoid late nighters."

Lucille fluttered her fake lashes toward Adam. "I'll come, but I can't stay long."

At the condo, the two bodyguards stayed in the hall and manned the front door. Lucille lingered for an hour of small talk over a couple of tequila sunrises then excused herself with a respectable kiss on Travis' cheek. "See y'all at Russell's office at noon."

Adam, Monica, and the senator remained together until after one consuming one drink after another. The host's cleverness turned to mindless foolishness as alertness slipped into lethargy. While Adam fought to stay awake, Travis continued to tell tall tales and talk about old times.

At one-thirty, Monica tapped her boss' shoulder. "We have a pretty heavy schedule tomorrow including a chamber of commerce speech in Dallas. Think we better wrap it up for tonight?"

Travis nodded. "Sure, sure." He attempted to rise from his chair, but faltered.

Adam reached toward him. "Here, let me give you a hand. I'm in a little better shape."

He lifted his friend to a standing position, helped him stagger into the bedroom and laid him across the bed fully clothed. He pulled off Travis' shoes, waited a few minutes then returned to the living room. "Think he'll be okay?"

"Poor guy can't hold his liquor, but not to worry, he'll be off and running in the morning."

Adam shrugged. "Terrific, but what say we put in a ten o'clock wake-up call to make sure?"

"I can handle that."

He placed his arm around Monica's thin waist and guided her out of the condominium. Adam shook a finger at the bodyguards. "Keep a close watch, fellas."

Tommy Joe removed a toothpick from his mouth. "Don't worry, Mr. Cain. One of us is here all the time."

Adam moved away a short distance. "Having an armed guard sit there all night really makes Travis look paranoid. Not exactly the image you want to portray for a guy who bills himself as a fearless crime fighter. I think they need to move inside or use electronic surveillance."

Monica nodded. "Good suggestion. We'll take that up at the meeting tomorrow. The security folks should be able to offer some options, too."

"Sounds like a plan."

She looked at him, held his eyes. "Would you like to come down to my condo?"

Adam paused only for a split second. "Very much."

At ten o'clock, he awakened to the alarm and stared at her like a guilty schoolboy. "Monica?"

She touched his lips. "Shh. Don't." She wiggled her finger toward the phone without opening her eyes. "Time to call Travis."

Adam punched the keys on the phone, but even after twelve rings, no one answered. "That's odd. Travis never picked up."

She put her arm across his chest. "Maybe he's in the shower. We'll try again in a few minutes."

After a hurried breakfast washed down by a couple of cups of strong black coffee, he picked up the phone again. Fifteen rings, and no response. "Doesn't he have an answering machine?"

"Usually." She glanced at the clock on the wall. "Well, it's ten-forty-five, and we're supposed to be at Russell's at noon. We better go get him up."

He followed her up the two flights of stairs to the senator's. Al sat alone at the front door. He moved his body back and forth in his seat like an old man in a rocking chair.

"Senator Hamilton leave?"

"Nope."

"Anyone go in?"

The big bodyguard continued to rock. "Nope."

Adam placed his lower lip between his teeth and pulled it back against them. "Let us in."

"Nope. I'm under orders not to disturb him."

Monica placed a hand on her hip. "Look, it's almost eleven, and he has a noon appointment. I'm responsible for getting him there. Now do as Mr. Cain says, and open that door. Now."

The burly man stopped rocking and stared. "But I ain't suppose to disturb him."

Adam's face burned. "He's not answering his phone. Open the door and let us in or you'll be unemployed by noon." Adam glared at the bodyguard.

Al held his gaze a moment then looked away. "All right already. I'll let you in."

Adam led Monica through the condo. Nothing seemed out of order. Half-empty glasses rested where they were left the night before.

"Travis? Travis! Where are you?" There was no answer. Adam ran his hand through his hair and made his way to the bedroom.

Acrid stomach acid welled up his throat and burned his mouth. He swallowed and waved Monica to stand back. "You wait here." He pushed the unlocked door. "Travis, come on now. Don't mess with my head."

He opened the door wider. The unmistakable smell of gas fouled his nostrils. His friend lay fully clothed and motionless in almost the exact position as the night before.

Monica entered the room. "Where's that gas coming from? She covered her nose and mouth.

"I don't know." Adam fumbled about the politician's neck for a carotid pulse and felt none. He placed his lower lip between his teeth and pulled it back against them then wiped his brow, trying to maintain a sense of composure.

From the living room Al shouted, "Is that stink gas?"

Adam got Monica by the arm and guided her out of the bedroom. "He's dead."

Her hazel eyes widened, filled with tears, and then shut tight. "Can't we do something?"

He put his arms around her shoulders and pulled her next to him. "He's been dead a while. I'm so sorry, there's nothing. Nothing at all we can do for him." He faced Al. "Call 911."

"Right. What about the gas?"

"I'll see if I can locate the source." Adam sat her down on the sofa, patted her back then eased back into Travis' room. A steady hissing spewed from the metal pipe that ran across the firebox. He removed the handkerchief from his breast pocket and turned it off.

He walked back into the living room with the handkerchief still in his hand. "Any other gas outlets you know of? We'd better check them." He knelt beside the living room fireplace.

"None I know of. I thought all these fancy places were all electric."

Adam twisted the valve tight to the right. He faced the guard. "For G-d's sake, man. Get moving, open some windows and the patio doors!"

Al went from window to window and door to door, opening each as wide as possible until a breeze flowed.

* * * * *

A few miles away in front of a convenience store edged between Guadalupe Street and Lamar Boulevard, Lieutenant John Anderson and his partner sat in silence in his black Camaro. He engaged in two of his favorite pastimes, sipping hot coffee and listening to the all channel scanner. After a long lull, it blared to life.

"Paramedics in route to 8401 Riverside Drive, apartment five-twelve. Possible homicide. Cars fourteen, eight, twenty-four, and thirty-seven, dispatch to the scene immediately."

Anderson slammed the cruiser into reverse, spun the wheels, and turned a tight circle.

"Where you going? She didn't call us."

"That's Travis Hamilton's address."

His partner snapped his fingers. "You're right."

Anderson placed the magnetized red light on the roof, laid a tire track and sped to the scene.

From the time he had convinced Hamilton to wear

that wire, he considered the senator a friend and comrade-in-arms. Pulling up to the building, he snaked his way around a ladder truck, a fire engine, an ambulance, and three squad cars.

On the sixth floor, he encountered one of Travis' bodyguards. "What's going on here?"

The man lowered his head. "Senator's dead."

"Where's your compadre?"

"Couple of doors down getting some shuteye."

Anderson shook his head is disbelief. "Why isn't he here?"

"Don't know. Ain't called him or nothing. What's the point? Senator's dead."

"Well, get down there and wake him up. I want to talk to the both of you. Where's the senator?"

The only person in the room Anderson didn't know stepped forward. "In the bedroom, officer."

"And who might you be?"

"Adam Cain, a friend. And you are?"

"Detective John Anderson." He flashed his badge. "Austin PD." Anderson looked around and made a mental note of those present. He pointed to a uniformed officer. "Make sure no one touches anything or leaves."

He walked to the bedroom and spent a few minutes examining Travis' body then checked the room. No signs of a struggle or violence, a spread covered the area beneath Travis' body and all four pillows remained at the head of the bed.

Within minutes, the forensics team arrived and went

to work. Anderson watched them do their job for awhile. "Who's on call for the ME's office?"

"Doctor Rogers."

Anderson cursed to himself then called the morgue to get the ME's home phone number. "Morning Doc, John Anderson here. I got an emergency."

"Detective, you know perfectly well there aren't any emergencies in my line of work."

"How about the death of a state senator with a strong smell of murder?"

"Well."

"Doc, I know it's Sunday, but don't screw things up like you did last time."

Silence followed. "Who is it?"

"Travis Hamilton. He'll be to the morgue shortly."

Anderson hung up the phone then set up in Hamilton's study, behind a huge, hand-carved oak desk with the Texas senatorial seal in the center. Putting his feet against the desk, he pushed back in the plush, brown leather executive chair.

He scanned his group of suspects and potential witnesses through the open study door. He called out to one of the uniforms. "Bring me Tommy Joe Smith."

The bodyguard came in and sat down in the side chair. His immense body bulged through the chair's slatted side openings.

"You here all night?"

"Yep."

"Where were you positioned?"

"Right outside the front door."

"Any other entries to the condo?"

The large man looked down at the floor. "Guess if you were Spiderman you could walk up the back wall of the building and slip in by the balcony."

Anderson wrote on his note pad. "How about coming over from the adjoining terraces?"

"They're separated pretty wide, but I guess if someone wanted to bad enough, maybe."

"What time did you leave?"

"Six this morning when Al took over."

"Who was there last night?"

The man shifted in the chair like a con under a spotlight. "Um. Lucille Robbins for about an hour and a half and then she left. Mr. Cain and Ms. Gutierrez stayed till one-forty-five before they shoved off. No one after that."

"You sure?"

The bodyguard's face reddened. "Of course, I'm sure. I didn't move all night, not even for a whiz. They was the only ones in the condo with Hamilton. Nobody come in or out before or after."

"You sure you didn't fall asleep?"

"Of course not. I ain't paid to go to sleep when I'm on duty."

"You may go now." He looked up from his note taking. "Send in Al."

The other security guard reiterated what had occurred that morning in painstaking detail.

After Anderson dismissed Al, he brought Monica into

the study. He softened his voice. "Where were you in the apartment when the body was found?"

Her red eyes moistened. "In the bedroom with Mr. Cain."

He pushed a small box of Kleenex in her direction. "So Cain wasn't in the room at any time without you?"

"I walked in behind him, pretty much. Travis looked like he was sleeping, then Adam told me he was dead."

Anderson stared her down. "Any time that Mr. Cain was in the room when you weren't there?"

She dabbed at her tears. "I guess, maybe, for a few seconds."

He tapped the end of his pencil. "Miss Gutierrez, you were pretty tight with the senator?"

"Yes, of course. As his chief legislative aide, I took care of a lot for him." Her soft voice carried her sadness, but remained steady. Her hazel eyes held no luster.

"Were you, involved sexually?"

"No. Definitely not." She folded her hands.

"Where did you go when you left the condominium last night?"

"To my apartment."

"Located where?"

"In this building two floors below."

Anderson turned his head to the side. "Can anyone confirm that?"

"Yes."

"Who?"

She moved her hands to the side arms of the chair and

took a deep breath, exhaling with a sigh. Her lips pursed, she closed her eyes for a second and then looked down at the carpet. "Mr. Cain spent the night with me. We left together to come check on Travis this morning when we couldn't reach him by phone."

"What was his relationship to the senator?"

"He and Travis were old friends and college buddies. He's very influential in the Dallas/Fort Worth area. The senator asked him to be a fund-raiser and advisor."

"That's all for now. But stick around."

She stood. "I haven't got anywhere to go anyway. My day's already shot."

Getting up from behind the great oak desk, Anderson arched his back and walked to the door of the study. He peered out at the suspects in the other room. "Mr. Cain? Please, come in."

The man strode into the room like he owned it. He pulled out a cigar. "Do you mind?"

"No." Anderson nodded toward the side chair.

"Am I a suspect, or are you questioning me as an old friend of the senator?"

"As far as I'm concerned, everyone is a person of interest at this time." He studied the man for a second while Cain lit the Cleopatra. His steady steel gray eyes gave no hint of intimidation. "Of course, if you want an attorney present, that's your prerogative and certainly appropriate."

"No. I have nothing to hide. Let's get on with it."

"Where were you last night?"

"At the Renaissance, of course, for the big announcement, then back here for a few celebratory drinks afterwards."

"And after you left the senator's condominium?"

"That's none of your business."

"Stop playing games. There's a probable murder of a very prominent person. Anything concerning your movements last night is relevant to my investigation."

Cain broke off a piece of ash from his cigar. "If you must know, I was with Monica Gutierrez."

"All night?"

"Yes."

"Was the senator in good shape before you left?"

"Travis never could hold his liquor. He got sloshed, and I helped him to bed. He was alive when I last saw him." Cain placed his lower lip between his teeth and pulled it back against them.

Anderson rose from his chair. "Did you notice anything that seemed strange or unusual?"

"Well, one thing kind of bothered me. In all the years I knew him, Travis never acted afraid of anything. Actually, he was a bit of a chance taker. Yet yesterday, he seemed very fearful and different than the last time we visited. Even when we were alone, there were guards constantly present. He seemed paranoid that someone was out to get him."

"Perhaps he had good reason and wasn't so paranoid after all."

Cain's steel gray eyes stared. "What do you make of

it? Was he murdered?"

"Don't rightly know yet. We're just getting started. If what you told me is correct, I don't think it possible that someone that drunk could've gassed himself. Besides, he was on too much of a roll to commit suicide. Maybe after a few years in the statehouse, but not on the way."

"Then who?

"Who, if, and why is for us to find out. Do we understand each other, Mr. Cain?"

He nodded.

Anderson gestured toward the door. "I have no further questions for you, but stay close."

"No can do." Cain snuffed out his cigar, grinding it into the ashtray. "I've got a business to run in Fort Worth."

"Then at least until the day after tomorrow?"

"Shouldn't be a problem."

"Good. You may leave then, but let me know how I can reach you."

"Okay."

"Then we're on the same page."

The man strolled out of the room. Anderson glanced at the ceiling while he collected his thoughts, then thumbed through Travis' Rolodex. Once he found Lucille's phone number, he called her and made an appointment to meet her at his office in an hour.

Next, he contacted Colonel Curtis Oliver, commander of B battalion of the Texas Rangers then Mark Allen, the Federal Bureau of Investigation Regional Director. Both men had worked closely with him on the money laundering case.

# 6 Going Home

What do you know? The senator gets buried tomorrow. Folks treat him like a real national hero. If you ask me, the man's importance is much exaggerated. I don't know why people pay him so much attention. Know what I mean?

After all, the guy was nothing more than a political hack who never would've amounted to anything if he hadn't married rich. Turned into a prince from a frog overnight.

Stupid also. Numero last in his law school class. Could've been plenty wealthy on his own. Just needed to do a couple of things a little bit different. My people didn't ask for much. Offered him a million dollars.

Instead? The self-righteous idiot rats us and some of his buddies out. Doublecross me and mine, and they're gonna get you sooner or later. Unless, of course you get yourself first. Could've staggered around and put the gas on himself for all you know.

Now the cops blame everything on some sort of conspiracy. Before long, the police will try to hang it on me or some of my people.

Guess I'll stay low for a spell. No use showing my hand and getting caught before I can finish my work.

I'll just slither into my cocoon and wait for a good target of opportunity.

*　　*　　*　　*　　*

Anderson shuffled the papers on his desk. Opening a large envelope from the medical examiner's office, he reviewed Travis' preliminary coroner's report. Death occurred from toxic gas inhalation and a blood alcohol twice that of the level for legal drunkenness.

He glanced at the headlines on the front page of the *Austin American-Statesman*.

Bill Declares Week Of Mourning For Hamilton State Buildings To Fly Flags At Half-Staff

He poured the cold black coffee left in his cup from earlier that morning into the sink. It matched his mood, and he really didn't feel like finishing the miserable tasting liquid anyway. He put the newspaper in a drawer and then drove to the Capitol building.

The senator's polished coffin lay in the center of the

capitol rotunda for public viewing. Attired in full dress uniform and armed with glistening rifles, soldiers and airmen from the Texas National Guard maintained a constant vigil over the fallen lawmaker. Every hour, the soldiers clicked their weapons three times on the marble floor, placed them on their opposite shoulders, walked at one-third pace and changed positions.

Anderson stationed himself in the shadows of a corner to observe the multitudes who passed by to pay homage. He searched for anyone who seemed out of place, but after several hours, turned surveillance over to his partner. Maybe he'd get lucky at the funeral.

The next day, a hearse transferred the senator's body to Saint Joseph's Episcopal Church. The great Gothic structure stood on a high hill surrounded by a forest that receded into a park and valley. Gray stones formed three spires that towered into the sky and became lost in the low clouds and mist. The dark light of sorrow cast its dreary spell upon the dimly lit pews packed with mourners.

Family members sat in the first three rows. Hamilton's mother looked like she was in shock, her frail body shook as she shuffled to her seat. Losing her eldest son to liver cancer just three years ago and now Travis' murder seemed too much for her to bear.

Monica held Mrs. Hamilton by the arm and tried to steady the old woman. A couple of cousins and a niece filled out the first row. To their right, the President and First Lady, Secretary Russell, Lucille, and other dignitaries whispered among themselves. Seeing the president surprised Anderson inasmuch as he ardently supported Governor Lovett.

The pipes of a grand old organ stretched from a nesting balcony to the very top of the church's high vaulted ceiling and doled out a sorrowful hymn.

Walking at a slow pace, the man officiating inched his way to the pulpit. The choir sang a psalm of David. "The Lord is my shepherd. I shall not want. He leadeth me to walk in green pastures—"

When they finished, the pastor grasped the edge of the wooden podium. "He who does evil will lie in hell with his evil." He lifted his head toward the top of the church as if to recognize G-d and the angels drifting among the wooden beams that held the grand arches in place.

He raised his hands toward them. "He who is righteous will rise to the kingdom of our Lord and spend all the days of eternity in the light of glory. In John twenty-two, verse twenty-one, Mary Magdalene told the disciples that she had seen the Lord.

"Then came Jesus who stood amongst them. To Thomas, the doubter, he said, 'Blessed are those who haven't had the chance to see me, but still believe.' Therefore, it is written that those who believe that Jesus is Christ, the son of G-d, will experience eternal life through his name."

Anderson had never thought of Hamilton as religious. He never discussed it before.

The pastor's voice softened for a moment and then rose with happy adulation. "As we mourn and worship today, rejoice, for Senator Travis Hamilton, loyal son, faithful husband, and servant of the people of Texas must truly be sitting at the side of the throne of sweet Jesus and smiling down upon us."

Odd to think of him in heaven now. Anderson looked up and wondered about Travis looking down. He intended to do the man proud, get to the truth and find his killer.

Next, Secretary Russell eulogized the fallen senator. "Travis embodied all those things that should be present in a great public servant. He was kind, honest, devoted, hard working and caring." Apparent sadness halted his voice. Anderson thought he might actually cry. "Although you now dwell in heaven with our Lord, we are sorry to lose you and your work for the people, my dear friend."

The pastor once again rose from his seat and stood behind the pulpit. "Do not repay evil with evil. Do not take revenge. Leave it for the wrath of the Lord. It is mine to avenge. It is my wrath, which I will visit upon those who do evil acts, so sayeth the Lord."

Texas and American flags draped the coffin. Six pall-bearers including Cain and Russell helped guide the casket into the hearse for the slow ride to the cemetery.

The long procession of motorcycle policemen, state troopers, and limousines filled with family and dignitaries eventually came to a stop next to a green-tented area.

Anderson wandered away as the graveside ceremony began. As he crisscrossed behind the crowd of mourners, a twenty-one-gun salute reverberated in the still air and the very heavens vibrated as a Texas Air National Guard F-16 squadron made a pass with one jet missing from the formation.

Before long he spotted Juan Gomez, a mid-level member of the Mexican Mafia. With his maroon jacket and yellow tie, the man stood out like a purple frog on a bright orange lilypad. Gomez attempted to blend in with a group leaving the funeral.

Moving toward a narrow pathway that bisected the cemetery, the gangster quickened his pace and then began to run. Anderson followed cautiously. He closed the distance a few feet at a time. The Mexican ducked in among the tombstones.

Anderson followed him to an isolated part of the cemetery, angled around and caught the thug by the back of his jacket. He slammed the bronze man's face against a large granite marker. "Why are you here?"

Gomez tried to move, but Anderson tightened his grip, scraping the man's face against the stone. "He was nice to us Mexicanos. No other reason."

He loosened his grip. "Yeah, right."

Gomez rubbed his face and neck. "Hey, man, what's wit you anyways?"

"If you don't give me a straight answer, I'll run you in. I got plenty of friends who'd love to take a crack at you."

"You can't do that. You ain't got no charges."

Anderson gave a little shove at the bulge under Gomez's jacket. "I bet that piece is stolen, and that alone is reason enough. Now, what are you doing here?"

The Mexican backed up a couple of steps and winced. "I come here for a look see."

"Yeah, about what?"

"Dunno. I like funerals."

"I'm getting impatient." Anderson pulled his piece then pointed the thing at the man's groin. "Like I said, what are you doing here?"

"You wouldn't."

"You hope." Anderson leaned in and tilted the revolver at a steeper angle and released the safety. "Real quick, tell me why."

"Okay, okay. The boss told me to keep an eye on Russell and anyone he talked to."

"You tell your boss, I'll be in touch." He let loose of the mobster.

*　　*　　*　　*　　*

Russell returned home soon after Senator Hamilton's funeral exhausted and deeply saddened at the loss of his friend and protégé. Shoot, Travis could've gone all the way to the White House.

Taking off his jacket, he opened the hall closet door. A white envelope fell from his shallow inside pocket. He picked it up. Funny, he didn't remember putting it there.

Suddenly, he recalled a slight mustached man bumping into his wife near the funeral's end. The force of the collision caused her to stumble. Could the guy have slipped it into his pocket as he reached out to break her fall? He opened it and took out a letter from the Las Cabañas Church and Orphanage.

> *Dear Mr. Secretary,*
>
> *We wish to thank you for your support over the past twenty-three years. Your funds have helped us to build new facilities throughout Mexico to help the needy. We no longer have financial requirements. However, we must once again ask for your support. It is essential that NAFTA pass Congress and be signed into law by the U.S. President. We solicit your support in this matter. NAFTA will help our supporters to import their products to the United States and Canada with much greater ease. This in turn will continue to help the children in our orphanages.*
>
> *May God go with you.*
>
>

Sincerely,
Father Diablo

Russell's arm dropped to his side and he crumbled the piece of paper in his hand into a ball.

"What's the matter, dear? Your face is almost white." His wife held his arm.

He shook his head. "Nothing, but this horrible day, I

imagine. And I just found a letter from some lobbyists. Wish they'd leave me alone."

7 Monica

Monica Gutierrez. A real good looker. What a great body and pretty face to boot. She's a smart, ambitious, and loyal broad. Emphasis on the word loyal.

Came to Austin as a student, used her talents as an intern, if you know what I mean, to work her way up as chief honcho for that slimeball Hamilton. Really admire that. Use your best assets in any way you can to accomplish your goals. Your brains, your body, whatever. If only she hadn't worked for the senator.

Now that Hamilton's gone I wonder what she'll do or where she'll go. But I feel she'll land on both feet, if my people and me don't get ahold of her first.

Bet she finds another politician and gets as much mileage as she can out of him. Then again, her blind ambition might cause her to go it alone. Wouldn't surprise me if she ran for political office some day. Perhaps even for governor or senator. Senator Monica Gutierrez. Has kind of a nice sound about it, don't you think?

She'd do a lot better job of it than her old boss. She knows how to manipulate things real good, and that's an advantage to any politician.

Know what? If that happens, she could become real useful.

*   *   *   *   *

Monica stood in the middle of her ex-boss' office on the first floor of the state capitol. Stacks of boxes and papers crowded the desks and carpet. She gathered one pile marked *Personal* to donate to the archives of the University of Texas at Austin.

Another set of documents would make a trip down the hall to Senator Coffee who was about to take over Travis' chairmanship of the Senate finance committee. A third stack would be sent to the State of Texas for storage. Helping with this arduous and tedious chore, several aides labored beside her like beavers gathering wood and ground cover to build their dam.

The Metroplex entrepreneur's entrance surprised her. She'd not heard a word from Adam Cain in more than two weeks.

He took off his Stetson. "Looks like quite a mess."

She raised an eyebrow, trying not to show too much emotion. "A lousy job, winding down things here."

He moved closer. "Must be pretty painful."

"One of the most difficult things I've ever had to do. Really have to push myself just to keep going."

Adam brushed his hand across his hat. "What are you going to do when your work at the capital is done?"

"Go back to Edinburg. Congressman Juarez wants me to run his district office for him. "She picked up a large box.

He stepped forward and grabbed it. "Here, let me help."

"Sure, that's great. Thank you."

He picked up another finished container. "Where does this one go?" She pointed, and he continued to help with the larger boxes. Before long, he came to the empty corner where Monica had retreated. "Look, I owe you an apology. Things have been a little bit screwy. Sorry I haven't called. Truth is, I haven't been able to get you out of my mind. How about dinner tonight?"

She nodded. "I'd love it."

At seven-thirty, he led her past Sixth Street's rock and roll clubs and through a thick crowd of tourists and college students to reach Louie B's. Adam's hand on the small of her back felt great. She really liked him and was glad he had returned to her life.

The host showed them to a table on the second floor. A candle flickered and made grotesque shadows of a vase of fresh flowers there. The conversation went easy enough, but she found herself hoping time would rush on.

Folks all around just seemed too happy for her mood.

Every now and then, she passed her fork through her lobster and pasta, but hardly ate. Nothing smelled or tasted right since the senator's death.

After dinner, Adam drove her home. At the front door of her condominium, she turned. "Do you mind if I don't invite you in tonight? I can't seem to get my head clear to do much of anything since Travis died." Maybe it was being with the one who shared the horrible experience so closely with her, but she couldn't shake her sadness. A tear spilled from her eye, but she didn't mean to cry.

He dabbed it gently then embraced her for a very long time. "I fly down to the border and Guadalajara often. Mind if I drop in from time to time?"

"No, not at all. I'd really like that."

Adam kissed her forehead then departed.

With the senator's office all packed up and cleared out, her official duties in Austin ended, she couldn't wait to leave. Though she hadn't seen or talked to Adam, he'd definitely been on her mind, especially as she boarded the plane home. She hoped that he would stop by like he said.

Her mother and two sisters met her at the McAllen Airport, and they shared a tearful reunion. She was happy to finally be back. Maybe not for good, but for a much needed rest-and-relaxation wallowing in the comfort of family. While she had enjoyed the importance of her work in Austin, she missed the Rio Grande Valley and the people she loved there.

The capital job permitted her to buy a nice home for

her mother, put one of her sisters through college, and enroll the other in a college-prep high school. Her time away had really aged her mom, though. She looked so tired and worn.

Poor Mama. She'd had a tough life losing her husband to tuberculosis and having three daughters to raise alone. Monica tried to help as much as she could, but her mother never got over it. At the tender age of fourteen, she vowed not to ever forget the sacrifices her parents made for their family.

Two weeks passed before she began to work again. The prospect of getting back in the swing of things excited her. Each day, her service to Congressman Juarez eased the sense of loss.

Working for him opened the opportunity to get out among the people of the Fifteenth Congressional District, renew old friendships, and get a good feel for the plight of Hidalgo County. She loved it. Wages remained low, unemployment high, and health services scarce for much of the citizenry, but she knew she could help to make a difference.

The legislator seldom returned home. Monica became his personal stand-in at christenings, large family functions, municipal events, union meetings and Hispanic heritage fiestas. In his stead, she also attended conferences for governors of neighboring Mexican States to discuss border issues.

Another enjoyment came in the form of Adam's brief visits that offered a respite from her busy and hectic public schedule. Quite often, she crossed into Mexico with him and relaxed at a small, isolated resort fifty miles away for private time far from political distractions.

Sixty-eight-year old Roberto Juarez had represented the Fifteenth District for more than twenty years. She knew he planned to retire in a few years. However, it surprised her after she'd been with him only three years that he asked her to fly to Washington, meet with him and some other party leaders.

Congressman Juarez sat behind an old weather-beaten desk in his small office in the Sam Rayburn Congressional Office Building. As she entered, he motioned for her to sit. Only Russell waited in the room with him.

"Monica, I've got terminal cancer and am going home next week to announce my retirement. I want to spend my last days with my family."

"Oh, Roberto. I'm so sorry." The idea of losing another supervisor to death caused such dread. She swallowed a dry lump in her throat. "How can I help? What can I do for you?"

The congressman closed his eyes and grimaced as though in pain. "There will be a special election in two months. Russell and I are looking for a person with strong convictions who knows the economic situation in the Valley and can influence others in the House to pass meaningful legislation."

She nodded, glanced at Russell then looked back to the congressman. "I'm happy to help with the transition.

Just tell me what needs to be done."

Russell smiled. "How do you feel about the North American Free Trade Alliance? Many congressmen from non-border states and Ross Perot of the Reform Party feel it will pull jobs away from us to Mexico and cause an increase in drug trafficking."

"Oh, I believe NAFTA will reshape the entire economy of the Rio Grand Valley. The rest of the country will hardly be affected, if at all." She scooted to the edge of her chair and waved a finger. "If Mexico becomes a major trade partner, it has to increase, not decrease, jobs in the long run."

Congressman Juarez leaned on his desk. "I like your answer. So then, do you think you could continue my strong support for NAFTA with all your heart?"

"Of course. If it helps our people, there can be no other answer."

Russell rose from his chair and offered his hand to Monica. "Then my dear, you are our choice to replace Roberto when he retires. Will you run for Congress?"

The question stunned her. "I don't know. I never ran for office before, or even considered it." She sat back and touched her chest. "I'm very flattered." She thought for a few moments. "I know we have the organization in place, but what about campaign funds?"

Congressman Juarez stood and grasped his chair. "Your friend Adam Cain has offered a substantial amount. Our support is powerful in the Valley. You shouldn't have any problem winning."

She paused and reflected a while longer then stood and smiled. "Then my answer is yes. I'd be honored to run for your place, Roberto."

Days after Congressman Juarez announced his retirement, Monica held a press conference to declare her candidacy. Friends and family jam-packed her alma mater, Edinburg High School. Congressman Juarez, now in a wheelchair, sat to the side of the dais.

Sister Magdaline Nicholas, a nurse who worked with impoverished children, introduced her. "I am so pleased to talk to you tonight about one of our very own." The nun smiled.

"When her father died, Monica Gutierrez worked hard to help her mother support her two younger sisters. All the time, she maintained an A average right here at Edinburg High. On a full scholarship to UT, she spread her wings and left us to make her way in this world. And made us proud.

"You all know what awful circumstances brought her home, but we were glad to have her back serving with our beloved Congressman Juarez. Today, she is running for Congress to continue his good works. Because she is aware of the people of this Valley, she knows their suffering, but shares their faith in G-d and for a bright future."

The spontaneous applause overwhelmed Monica. She rose and moved to the podium. "It feels so good to be home with mi familia. All my family." She spread open her arms and turned to include everyone in the building.

"Here, we are all familia." More applause erupted.

"I remember how my poppa and momma struggled as tenant farmers and how many there are of you who can't find work today. Too many of our families live in rundown houses and have too little to eat.

"The Fifteenth District has the highest unemployment rate in the state of Texas. Even when you find work, it is almost impossible to get there because either there is no public transportation, or your cars can't drive through the muddy mess they call roads.

"Well, mis amigos, I have a way out. It is five little letters. NAFTA. Say it with me."

They repeated. "NAFTA, NAFTA."

"Say it again."

And so they did.

She moved her hand up and down and then pointed to her audience. "This is the Fifteenth District's one way out of the poverty cycle. Hidalgo County will become the center point of all goods coming up from Mexico for distribution throughout the United States, and with it, we will develop a new source of good jobs, more suitable homes, improved schools, and a better chance for mi familia."

Several in her audience stood and whistled their approval over the thunderous clapping. She smiled and waved both hands over her head.

With all the funding and party support, the election should have been very easy to win, but Monica took nothing for granted and crisscrossed the entire district, going door to door and visiting almost every constituent.

Her opponent, Oscar Miller, left no stone unturned either. A tipster had informed him of Monica and Adam's liaisons in Mexico, and he went public with the information, claiming he could produce statements from the resort owner and some of his staff.

Monica refused to answer his accusations. "Miller can't beat me on the issues. So he's trying to slander me," she repeated in more TV interviews and newspapers than she could keep track of.

Somehow, the day Miller's witness was to confirm the affair, the man was nowhere to be found. He didn't show up for the interview. Left with unsubstantiated claims, her opponent looked like a fool. The election was a slam-dunk.

She won by a landslide of seventy-eight percent. Keeping her promise to Congressman Juarez and Secretary Russell, as soon as she arrived in Washington, she worked hard to convince other representatives of the importance of NAFTA to their constituencies.

When the trade alliance passed in Congress, her dream for the valley began to take hold.

8 The Trap

In life, contacts and allies are very important. I've got the best associates and colleagues all over the world. Major corporations, governments, organizations, individuals, crime syndicates. They belong to me, and I control them.

My biggest bang for the buck is in Mexico. Actually, I owe them a lot. In a way, they are the very ones who helped me get started. They're bloodsuckers, you know.

Been paying them back for a long, long time. Any way you dice it, the price has been hefty to pay for what they did, and it never seems to end. Can't ever seem to satisfy them folks. No matter how much they get, they keep asking for more dinero.

On the other hand, whenever I need a big favor or the cartel to do a job, I can count on them to get it done and leave no proof behind. You know what I'm talking about;

one hand washes the other.

That's life. It's done all the time.

Don't trust them too much, but they're the best I got. With governments, sometimes too many people start talking.

I do plenty for them, too. You know, a man once said, "From all evil comes some good." I know they transport drugs and illegals, but hey, they gotta make a living, and besides, they do plenty for orphanages, churches, old folks, and hospitals.

Got to always watch my back with them, though. I'm like the shark, and they're the suction fish. The shark gets the big kahunas, the suction fish hang on and get the scraps. The shark does all the heavy work, and the little ole suckers lay back and get fat and enjoy life. And, most of the time, don't become dinner.

The idea is to let them help you, but you really need to watch your ass. I'm going to surprise them folks. Got connections they have no idea about.

It's time I shut off my water faucet to them and stop bleeding pesos. Even so, I'll have them around to do some of my dirty work. The suction fish will get the shark this time around and then find another to hook onto. Just wait and see.

*　　*　　*　　*　　*

Guadalajara, 1994

Pablo Menendez bent down and kissed his mother on the forehead. She looked at him from her wheelchair with blank eyes. "Adios, Julio. Will you come tomorrow?"

He shook his head and turned toward the nurse. "She was so beautiful and alive. Now she can't even remember who I am. It breaks my heart." He leaned in close to the woman. "Change her more often. She stinks."

The nurse opened her mouth, but Pablo silenced her with his eyes. Putting his arm around his mistress' waist he guided her out of his mother's home. His chauffeur opened the Cadillac's back door.

The limousine wove its way through the streets of Guadalajara. Pablo liked the spacious modern metropolis filled with Spanish colonial architecture. If only his mother could still enjoy it.

He pulled his mistress close. The limo's smoky windows hid him, but he was still seventy miles away from his fortress in the mountains near Anahulco. He regretted leaving his mother after such a short visit, but he had work to do. American International Aviation, a worldwide airplane service and short-haul company and the perfect front for his drug trafficking, needed his attention.

He smiled as he passed the Cabañas Church and Orphanage. Melodic mariachi music and the smell of fresh roasting peppers drifted through the air from the

Plaza Tapapita across the street. Pablo loved the fact that he had donated more than a million dollars to this church and home for abandoned children in his mother's name. The kids sure didn't care where the money came from, and neither did he.

That evening, the meeting with his lieutenants exhausted him, but after a few hours he identified several suspects responsible for leaking information to the authorities. After a late dinner, and some more lovemaking, he fell into a deep sleep.

*　　*　　*　　*　　*

Drug Enforcement Agent Luis Cardona gave a coded message to a security officer in front of a dilapidated storehouse in the old warehouse district of Guadalajara. The man led him to an open elevator loft and pressed a button to the fourth floor.

A row of containers stacked in haphazard fashion leaked a petroleum distillate that burned his nostrils. Steady dripping water from the roof formed small puddles that had dried around the edges, leaving a musty residue on the floor.

Cardona reached a well-lit, windowless area in the back of the building. Eight men sat around a table laden with documents and two large maps marked into quadrants. Leaning firmly against the desk, he spoke in a soft, but firm voice.

"Welcome to Operation Ricardo. Every man here was

picked for his expertise and precision. Each of you knew Ricardo Hernandez. Pablo Menendez and his cartel tortured and murdered our agent. Most of Guadalajara's police are on his payroll, and they'll never do anything to bring Ricardo's killers to justice."

He searched the eyes of those present. "In two hours, Menendez will be informed that his mother was taken to the University of Guadalajara Medical Center with a stroke. He'll use caution, but will go to the hospital to visit the old lady."

Silence filled the room.

"Menendez operates from a headquarters on a high mountain between Amatlan and Anahulco. Only one set of roads leads from his base to the hospital."

Cardona traced the route on the map with a laser beam pointer. He stopped the prick of light at the intersection of México Federal Highway 70 and Jalisco State Highway 29.

"We'll trap him here, just before the connection. Three minutes before the arrival of Menendez's limousine, we'll jackknife a gas trailer-truck on the Highway 29 side. Friendly operatives will create a traffic jam half a mile away."

He targeted a short, well-built man sitting at the opposite end of the table. "Jeff, you'll drive the tanker. We'll position the truck just three minutes before the Menendez vehicle reaches the blockade point. Detonation will occur within one minute, so get out of there fast.

"With a little luck, we'll surprise the driver and force him to come to a complete stop before he can recover. During that time, Ron and José will approach the limousine from either side on motorcycles and take out the driver and front-seat bodyguard. Bart will come in from behind and do away with the muscle in the back seat. He and Jaime will snatch Menendez."

Cardona placed a large picture of the drug lord on top of the maps. He thumped the photo several time with his index finger. "Get a good look. This man ordered the hit on Ricardo. We want him alive, if at all possible. We want him to stand trial. Understand?"

"Yes, sir," the others answered in unison.

*   *   *   *   *

Ringing several times, Menendez's secure phone awakened him. He disengaged from his mistress' warmth, rubbed his eyes and picked up the receiver. "Hello."

"Jefe, your mother has a problem."

"You disturb me at one in the morning to tell me my mother has a problem?"

"Jefe, she had a stroke tonight, slipped into a coma and is near death."

He passed his hand through his greasy disheveled hair. "Díos mío. When did this happen?"

"Less than an hour ago. The doctor's sent her to the University of Guadalajara Medical Center."

Menendez rose from his bed and paced. "Why didn't they take her to our private hospital?"

"I don't know, Jefe. She was very sick, and her neurologist wanted her to go to the university."

His mind raced. Was this a scheme to attack him through his family? Or had someone in the government gone honest? "Did you send any of our men with her?"

"Yes, of course. I also contacted your brother in Mexico City. He'll be on the first flight in the morning."

Menendez glanced at the floor. His jaw muscles tightened. "Anyone contact Dr. Suarez?"

"No."

He sat down on the bed and paused for a few seconds. "Call him. Tell him what happened to my mother and have him come to my home. He and I will go to the hospital together."

"What if she gets worse?"

"I'll have to take that chance." He hung up the phone.

His mistress removed her hand from his back. "What's happened?"

"My mother had a stroke, and they took her to the University Hospital."

Getting up from the bed, she began to get dressed.

"Oh, my love. Let's go now. Will she be okay?"

"We go nowhere, mi novia. My enemies would expect me to react exactly in that manner."

Tears formed in the corners of her green eyes. "But, Pablo! What's wrong with you? Your mother could pass away. And without you seeing her. G-d will curse you for that."

He grabbed her by the arm and threw her onto the bed. "Shut up. Someone's setting a trap. I know it in my gut."

She stared with pleading eyes. "And what if she dies?"

He glared until she looked away. "Then I will have one more thing to answer for."

In the quiet of his library, he poured a shot of Tequila Oro, sagged into his leather chair, and formed a contingency plan.

* * * * *

As soon as he received the call, Suarez slipped into his well-worn white suit. Within the hour, he drove his Buick Le Sabre onto the steep narrow road that led to his friend's fortress and stopped at the front gate. He blinked his lights four times in rapid succession. Spotlights from high on the wall bathed his car and made surrealistic shadows against the craggy terrain. For a moment, the glare partially blinded him.

Then the massive steel gate receded into the concrete wall, and he drove though. He parked in the circular driveway in front of Pablo's villa. Two men armed with automatic weapons walked to either side of his car.

One gestured toward the house with his gun. "El Jefe wants to see you right now." The bodyguard led him into the central patio near the pool. "Sit down. He will be with you soon."

Suarez sat in a large, well-padded green and white lounge chair.

After a few minutes, Pablo appeared and embraced him. "We're like brothers, is that not true?"

Queasiness hit his stomach. He folded his arms against his chest and studied his friend's face very carefully. He suspected their conversation would take a negative turn. "True, we are. However, I don't think you made me drive all the way up here at two in the morning to tell me that you love me like a brother."

Scratching his head, Pablo smoothed his hair. "No, I didn't. What do you know about my mother?"

"Nothing. Is something wrong?" He took a step back.

"Díos mío, then you didn't know she was taken to the University Hospital unconscious this evening?"

"No one informed me of this. Why not? I can go to the hospital now and check on her."

"Good idea, amigo, but I've got a better one."

The queasy feeling returned to the pit of Suarez's stomach. His "brother" had cooked up some crafty scheme. "I don't think I'm going to like it, but then I don't have any choice, do I?"

"No." Pablo offered a wry smile. "Let's just say it would not be in the best interest for your health to do anything contrary to my wishes."

At three-thirty in the morning, Pablo's long shiny Cadillac flashed its lights three times. The huge metal gate opened, creating a small aperture for the car to leave the compound, and then closed. The Caddy circled around the mountain on Menendez's private gravel road toward Jalisco State Highway 29.

*   *   *   *   *

Luis Cardona sat in his truck command post when his radio crackled.

"Momma, Eagle. Do you copy?"

Grabbing his mike, Cardona hit his send button. "Eagle, I copy."

"The chicken and two roosters just rolled out of the coop."

He took a deep breath. "You sure?"

"Affirmative, make and license check out. Subject positively identified."

"Thank you, Eagle. Momma will prepare breakfast."

"Baby one and two, do you copy?" He pushed the top of a small flashlight to illuminate a booklet of maps hanging from his console.

"One copies."

"Baby two's gotcha."

"The chicken's left the coop. Confirm passage on visual. Babies three through six, do you copy?"

Each replied in turn.

Cardona surveyed the previously marked positions while he waited. Ten minutes crawled by before another message came through. "Baby one. Subject just passed my position. Estimate arrival at twelve. I repeat, twelve minutes. Do you copy?"

"Affirmative." Cardona marked his map then peered into the dark of the evening. A thick layer of clouds filled the sky and obstructed the moon. His watch's iridescent hands read three forty-five. He steeled himself like a precision machine ready to spring into action, no emotions, not a quiver. No rise in pulse.

The radio once again interrupted the nocturnal silence. "Baby two. Subject just passed my checkpoint. Estimated time of arrival to your position five, I repeat, five minutes."

"Head's up everyone. Subject's five minutes from the construction site. Three, position your vehicle now and then get out."

Cardona retrieved his night vision binoculars and focused on the petroleum truck moving into place. The driver braked and the truck angled across the highway so that the tank obstructed the highway with the cab jackknifed behind it. The agent leaped from the cab and ran.

Cardona turned his attention up the road. The Cadillac approached at a steady speed. Several hundred yards before the limo reached the truck, he pressed the detonator button. The tanker erupted with a loud blast that shook the stillness of the night, casting a large wall of flames in all directions at once, as though hell created itself on earth.

*　*　*　*　*

The force of the explosion jolted Doctor Suarez in the rear seat of the limousine. The chauffeur locked the brakes and the automobile slid sideways toward the raging inferno. The forward energy carried the limo closer and closer to the fireball.

The car finally came to a halt just before it hit the wreckage. Through the smoke, carnage, and debris, two motorcyclists dressed in black appeared on either side of the limousine at the same time. The driver shifted into reverse. Suarez turned around. A red pickup truck pulled behind them, blocking any escape.

The cyclists came to an abrupt stop. One aimed a machine pistol at the driver's head. The chauffeur's window exploded, shattering into small shards of glass. A bullet hit the large man in the left temple and another in the neck.

Blood gushed in a violent stream from an artery. Small bits of brain tissue and skull splattered the car. The chauffeur fell forward onto the steering wheel and the horn echoed with a monotonous resonance.

Wheeling around, the bodyguard in the passenger's seat aimed his weapon at the assailant. Before he could get a shot off, the black-clad man on the opposite side of the car placed a bullet in his head just above his right ear. The brawny man fell limp and slumped on top of his fallen colleague.

Smashing through the rear window glass, a black hand reached in and opened the door. Suarez felt the cold steel revolver against his skull.

"Señor, scoot over to the door. Keep your hands where I can see them, and get out."

He peered out the window. Two other men trained their weapons on him. "If you wanted to kill me, you would have done so by now. That makes you government, but from which country?"

He pulled himself across the seat to the outside and offered no resistance.

* * * * *

Cardona looked over the prisoner for a few seconds. He ordered the man's head covered and hustled him to a second truck. Surveying the operational field, he activated his microphone. "I've got him, babies. Disperse as planned." He jammed the truck into gear. The wheels kicked up a cloud of dust as he headed off cross-country.

A red glow still illuminated the evening sky and reflected in Cardona's rearview mirror. The wail of fire engines echoed in the distance. The entire operation took less than five minutes.

The beating rhythm of helicopter blades sliced through the humid, foul smelling air as they arrived at the pickup site. The first Bell Jet Ranger landed just a few seconds later. Three DEA agents shepherded the prisoner onto the chopper. It took off without incident.

Cardona and his prisoner flew south for one hundred and twenty miles and then landed at a crude airstrip near the pacific coastal town of Chamela in a low-lying area near the Rio San Nicholas.

As the sun rose and shimmered like little pieces of glass on the breaking waves, a lone unmarked U.S. Air Force C-130 skimmed in low over the Pacific Ocean and put down at the airfield at Chamela. Cardona and his still hooded prisoner boarded, then as quickly as the cargo plane landed, it took off again, rising over the craggy terrain to the east and then turning south.

When the aircraft reached cruising altitude, the largest of the three agents leaned over the prisoner, braced against the side of the plane, and thrust his face to within an inch of the captive. "Pablo Menendez, on behalf of the government of the United States of America, I hereby arrest you for the murder of United States Drug Enforcement Agent Ricardo Hernandez.

"Under our law, you have the right to remain silent. Anything you say can and will be used against you in a court of law. You have the right to representation by an attorney. If you cannot afford one, the court will appoint one for you."

The suspect took a deep breath and sighed. "Gentlemen, you have made a terrible mistake. You have arrested the wrong man. My name is Doctor Humberto Suarez y Garcia."

The agent shook his head. "Nonsense. We took all your papers. Your driver's license, credit and business cards all identify you as Pablo Menendez."

"Unfortunately, you still captured the wrong man. I'm a physician and not Menendez. I'm a Mexican citizen.

You have no right to kidnap me." Suarez shook his head.

Cardona carefully studied his prisoner's face and body. "Señor, pull down your pants."

Suarez frowned and narrowed his eyes. "You are as crazy as you look with one blue and one brown eye. What's up with that?"

"Pull down your pants!"

The prisoner's face turned crimson. "I'll do no such thing."

The DEA agent grabbed the prisoner's arm. "Easy or hard? Your choice."

Cardona calmed his voice. "Either you pull down your pants, or we'll do it for you."

The man hesitated then loosened his belt. His pants fell to the floor.

"Now your undershorts."

He frowned, but dropped his shorts down to his knees.

"Hold it right there." Moving closer, Cordona inspected the man's buttocks. He sighed and pursed his lips. "We screwed up! This guy looks just like Menendez, but we've got the wrong man! The big kahuna has a tattoo of a fire-breathing dragon on the right cheek of his ass."

"Do we get rid of this guy?" an agent asked too loudly. Cardona stared at the doctor. The man trembled. Beads of sweat appeared on his forehead. "No, we'll figure out what to do when we reach the States."

The C-130 continued south over the Pacific Ocean. Just before Juchitan, the aircraft turned east over a narrow, sparsely populated area of Mexico and headed for Homestead Air Force Base near Miami.

The Connection

"KLRD in Dallas/Fort Worth, our up-your-tailpipe traffic report: there's some patchy ice on the bridges and overpasses, especially along Stemmons Freeway, at LBJ and Central and the Fort Worth Mixmaster."

Jackson Freed rolled over in his bed and hit the snooze-alarm button. Ten minutes later, the radio turned itself on again and blared an early morning shock jock sports show. He hit the reset button once more, but this time, the radio failed to shut off. Rising onto one elbow, he peered out the window to a gray, dreary day.

But, hey, he was glad Haddie awakened before him and promised breakfast. The scent of fresh-brewed French vanilla coffee, and the unmistakable sizzle of frying bacon made his morning more tolerable. Good old Haddie. Finding her had changed him into him a happy man. He smiled.

Before her, three marriages ended in divorce because he could not be content with just one woman. A rapid succession of mistresses followed, and his philandering led to four children out of wedlock. He supported all of them and spent considerable time with each in spite of his consuming schedule.

His favorite was his youngest son, Robbie, six years old. The boy captivated his heart. Of the four siblings, Robbie alone resided with Jackson.

He met Haddie at an upscale Fort Worth bar. Her flowing red hair caught his attention the moment he laid eyes on her. He remembered sitting next to her and ordering two drinks.

"What's your name, good looking?"

"Hadassah Wesson."

"Sounds like a Jewish charity." He moved his chair closer and digested her beauty.

"My momma named me from the Bible. Good friends call me Haddie."

He smiled. "Am I good enough to be your friend?"

Cocking her head, she permitted her hair to fall below her shoulders almost down to her waist. "I suppose that has yet to be seen. But yes, you may call me Haddie."

Jackson never knew if it was his wit, charm, or wealth that impressed her most. For sure it wasn't his portly build, but he took her home that first night four years ago and never looked back.

He ate his breakfast, dressed in a navy blue suit, topped his head with his favorite white Stetson, and began the commute to his office in downtown Fort Worth. He turned onto Main Street and then through Sundance Square.

He loved the old red light district especially since the billionaire Bass family resurrected it and transformed it into a respectable town center. Reflective glass skyscrapers surrounded brick streets, antique shops, restaurants, clubs, theaters, and a performing arts center.

Jackson pulled into a multilevel parking garage that connected to the Sundance Towers office buildings. The vast majority of his legal associates, paralegals, and secretaries had not made it into work yet.

However, his personal secretary sat at her desk in front of his office transcribing notes. Like the postman, neither rain, nor sleet, nor hail nor ice could keep her from her appointed task.

Jackson surveyed the mostly empty office. "Where is everybody?"

She shook her neatly coiffed head. "Didn't you notice? There's been an ice storm. I doubt anyone else will show."

"Any messages?"

Tearing a pink slip from a pad, she handed it over. "Just one. A José Perez from Guadalajara."

He looked at the memo and tossed it back on her desk. "Did he say what he wanted?"

"No. Wouldn't tell me much. Just said he needed to talk to you about a very urgent matter. Said you should call him as soon as you got in."

Lighting up a large cigar, Jackson took a couple of puffs, waited for the button to light up then lifted the receiver. "Hello, Mr. Perez, what can I help you with?"

"Mr. Freed, I have an urgent problem. I'm in a position to make a quick resolution very attractive to you."

"I'll be the judge of that. What do you want?"

"I'm vice president of American International Aviation. Our president, Pablo Menendez, asked that I call you to discuss a legal matter."

Jackson pushed back in his plush brown leather chair and paused for a moment. Menendez. Wasn't he the head of one of the largest drug cartels in Mexico? "What kind of legal matter?"

"A friend of our company was kidnapped from Guadalajara by DEA agents and flown to your country."

"Where?"

"Miami."

"Well, I'm in Texas. What do you think I can do for you in Florida?" He inhaled his cigar and slowly let the smoke curl out of the corners of his mouth.

"Don't play with me, Mr. Freed. You litigate cases all over the United States. You are one of the best attorneys in the country."

"Wrong, Mr. Perez. I am the best."

"I stand corrected."

Jackson leaned forward with his elbow on top of his solid white oak desk. "Why don't you hire a Miami attorney? They have plenty of good legal minds in Florida."

"Last time our people there handled a case for us they messed it up. Cost us a great deal of money. We wish you to take the lead in this case. Dr. Humberto Suarez is very important to Mr. Menendez, and he wants no mistakes this time around. Can you handle this for us, Mr. Freed?"

Jackson raised an eyebrow. "Tell you what, Perez. I'm very uncomfortable negotiating over the telephone. I'll send my chief investigator, Steve Shelton, to talk to you in person. If he feels it's appropriate for us to represent your friend and can make suitable financial arrangements with you, then," Jackson paused, "we go from there."

The silence on the other end indicated the possibility that Perez either had something else to consider or perhaps the drug lord was in the room. "One way to explore the matter. How can we identify him?"

"I'll call you with his flight number and time of arrival. Look for a tall thin guy with a large hooked nose. He'll be wearing an olive green suit and a gaudy tie."

*   *   *   *   *

Steve Shelton arrived a few minutes after eleven, and was ushered into Jackson's office. "You wanted me?"

The portly lawyer glanced over his reading glasses that perched halfway down his nose. "Want to get out of this weather?"

He knew it was a loaded question, but— "You got that right. Almost froze out there." Steve sat down.

"I need you to go to Guadalajara."

"What's the occasion?"

"Apparently, the DEA picked up one of Pablo Menendez's associates in Mexico and transported him to Miami. Perez wants us to represent the poor slob."

Steve rose from his chair and approached his boss' desk. "What else do you know about the deal?"

"Not much. Thought it imprudent to talk about such matters on the phone. Get to Guadalajara and get a feel for the situation."

A part of Steve listened as the lawyer outlined the details, but the biggest part of him wondered if this was an elaborate ruse. He hated doing business with the Mexican Mafia.

"You're dealing with dangerous folks here. Keep that in mind." The lawyer flicked off an inch of cigar ash. "I don't want them using you as a security deposit."

* * * * *

Just like Jackson said, the cartel's pickup man met Steve as he deplaned. The chauffeur drove him to a large multi-story office building in the heart of the city where he met with Perez and several high-level executives from American International Aviation. To his surprise, the cartel leader never entered into the negotiations.

Steve gathered as much pertinent information as possible about Doctor Humberto Suarez's abduction, his relationship to the cartel, and the assassination of DEA agent Hernandez. Then he negotiated the financial agreement with the aviation executive in the event that Jackson agreed to represent their compadre.

He returned to Fort Worth early the next evening and met up with his boss at Risky's. The attorney loved their ribs. Steve filled in his over-sized friend on the events leading to the death of Hernandez, the capture of Suarez, and the man's relationship to the cartel.

Jackson slathered butter on a piece of grilled Texas toast, then slugged down half a mug of Coors. Soon the waiter arrived at the table with a large portion of ribs, brisket, and sausage as strong scents of mesquite and barbecue sauce wafted through the air.

"You know, Steve, they tried a similar case in California a few years ago." Jackson licked his fingers. "A Mexican obstetrician named Robales was kidnapped by a U.S. law enforcement agency for allegedly aiding in the torture and death of an agent. They proved the case, but ended up with a hung jury."

He drained his beer and signaled the waiter for another. "The federal judge hearing the case refused to grant bail and ordered the man held for a new trial. However, the physician's attorneys petitioned an appellate court, which held that the manner in which the law-enforcement officers took the man into custody·was illegal because he wasn't a United States citizen and the Mexican government never consented to the arrest."

Jackson stuffed in another bite. "The upper court threw out the case and sent the accused home."

"Guess that means we'll take the case?"

"Depends what kind of deal you worked out."

Steve finished off a rib and tossed the bone onto his plate. "Perez promised to deposit a retainer of half a million drawn from American International Aviation into your account in the First Colonial International Bank of Miami."

He picked up another one. "They'll set you up with a suite at the Miami Intercontinental, and you can work out of their Miami attorney's office. Plus, I got an additional forty-five thousand a week if the trial extends beyond two weeks." Steve grinned, folded his arms, and nodded.

"I don't have a bank account in Miami."

"You do now."

Jackson tapped the table a couple of times with his hand. "When can you confirm the money?"

"Once you accept."

"What about travel arrangements to Miami?"

"Perez knows you like to fly your own plane. He'll pay for your fuel. You fly into Tamiami Kendall Executive Airport on the southwest edge of Miami."

Jackson's eyes narrowed. "Why there?"

"Our new friends have a subsidiary called Oro Express. They want you to hangar your plane there. They'll have a limousine at your disposal twenty-four hours a day."

"Don't like landing that far out. Never heard of the field. Sounds way too isolated."

Steve pushed his chair closer and leaned over the table. "Perez claims it's a large executive airport in a well-populated area with two runways longer than seven thousand feet, and a tower that's open till midnight. He also claims the Metro Dade Police Department headquarters some of their helicopters there."

Appearing at the table, the waiter smiled. "Can I get you anything else? How about another beer?"

"No, we're fixin' to leave." Jackson pulled a credit card from his wallet and handed it to the server.

"Do you want me to go down to Miami with you?"

"Nah, I'm thinking I'll need you back in Guadalajara."

10 Plans

Early the next morning, Jackson returned to his downtown office. As usual, his secretary had arrived before him. He barely acknowledged her and walked into his office. Behind his desk, he lit up a dark Havana cigar, inhaled and let out a thick cloud of smoke.

He called out in a thundering voice, "Get Perez on the phone for me."

Picking up the receiver, he leaned backward, took another drag on his cigar, and blew out a grayish-white halo. "Hello, Mr. Perez. Jackson Freed here in Fort Worth. Mr. Shelton and I discussed the arrangements of our deal last evening. I'll take your case under the conditions specified in your agreement. How soon can you make the financial arrangements?"

"Two hours suit you?"

He looked down at his Rolex. "Fine, once I have

confirmation—"

"Don't you trust us, Mr. Freed?"

He smiled. "Of course, Mr. Perez. However, business negotiations conducted at a distance makes confirmation both prudent and necessary."

"Then I assume we have a deal."

"If all arrangements are made satisfactorily, then we do have us a deal. I'll arrive in Miami on Thursday at fifteen hundred hours." Jackson made an entry on his computer.

"Good, a limousine will pick you up at the airport."

"One other thing. I never travel alone. My girlfriend always goes with me."

"No problem. We'll make sure you both are well taken care of."

Jackson returned home after work, feeling comfortable that he had a distinct advantage because of the appellate decision in the Robales case. The government might stall and maneuver, but in the end, legal precedent would determine the outcome of the trial.

He drove up the steep driveway to his palatial home. Haddie waited at the door, her curvaceous figure silhouetted against the glazed crystal entryway. Jackson and she embraced with firm tenderness, and he kissed her, tasting the sweetness of her lipstick.

Just then Robbie bounded down the stairs. "Daddy, Daddy! Haddie, Haddie! Mrs. Herrin took me to the zoo."

Jackson and Hadassah instantaneously disengaged except for their hands, which remained clasped. He pulled the boy toward him with his free hand and hugged him. "Tell me about it. Sounds like a great day."

"I saw lions and tigers and elephants and ate hot dogs and popcorn and ice cream."

"Lucky you don't have a tummy ache." He walked Haddie and his son to the dining room and ate dinner. In spite of excesses at the zoo, Robbie put away a hefty meal.

At eight o'clock, the nanny escorted the boy to his room. Haddie and Jackson soon followed upstairs, tucked him in, kissed him good night, then returned to the living room.

He slipped his arm around Haddie's shoulder and pulled her close to him on the couch. "Hadassah, do I have a deal for you." His voice was playful and soft.

"Jackson Freed, I know all about you and your deals." She gave him a gentle shove in the side.

"I'm serious. How'd you like to go to Miami? I've got a case down there. Don't think it'll take very long. While I'm in court, you can swim, shop, whatever. We'll be able to spend the nights together. Just the two of us, all by ourselves."

Her eyes narrowed. "What about Robbie?"

"He'll be fine staying at home with Mrs. Herrin."

"Sounds good to me." She sealed the deal with a kiss.

11 Anderson's Dilemma

I like that detective. A nice guy, but he doesn't have a clue. He tries to solve a crime by looking at everything systematically. Only he goes off in the wrong direction. Wrong way, Anderson. That's what I'll name him.

I suppose I could leave a hint or two. Then again, he might catch me and my amigos.

I'll feed him a little bit of information here and there, but only to throw him off the track. Actually, I'll lead him around by the nose. Sad part? He won't have the faintest idea.

So far, he hasn't caught on. Has no idea as to all the people involved. My guys play a real good game of deception.

He's really grasping at straws. Political considerations, you know. If he doesn't come up with something solid soon, bet they'll pull in someone else to work the case. That'd be bad for both of us, ruin my little cat and mouse game.

The cat runs here. The mouse runs there.
The mouse is here, there, and everywhere.
But the big bad pussycat can't see him.

See how much fun my game is? Like Mexican jumping beans beneath three shells. Now you see them, now you don't.

Ha, ha, ha. Makes me feel so good.

*　　*　　*　　*　　*

"Captain wants to see you."

"Not again." John Anderson closed his eyes. Deep down, he knew his supervisor had gotten caught up in the politics of the high profile case. He didn't like it one bit, but strategized how to handle it.

He opened his boss' door. Avoiding eye contact, the huge lawman peered down at a folder on his desk. "Have a seat, John. Be right with you."

He moved a chair closer to the paper-covered desk.

"What's going down, cap?"

The man closed the file. "Same old problem, John. That young snot from the governor's office called again." The older man wrinkled his nose then mocked the aide. "You don't even have a prime suspect, much less any kind of case on the Hamilton murder."

Anderson resisted saying what he wanted to.

"I know things have been hard, Shelly Sue running off with that lobbyist, leaving you with a kid and all, but we have got to move this case forward."

"What do you want? I'm doing the best I can. My personal life is under control since my dad and his wife moved down from Ohio."

"That's great, John, but I need results."

"It's a complicated case, boss. May take years to solve."

He pushed the file in Anderson's direction. "Maybe we ought to put the task force under the lead of another lieutenant. Maybe we need a fresh approach."

Anderson's face warmed. What an ungrateful SOB to even propose taking him off the case after all his hard work, the hours he'd put in. He took a deep breath. "What do you mean, new approach? I'm working with Colonel Oliver, and the FBI's been no help."

He took another deep breath. "The crime scene was entirely clean: no fingerprints, no tracks from vehicles around the building, nothing on the security tapes, no aircraft entering the area. No one living in the building saw anything.

"We're working what we have, boss. That's what an investigation is all about, following leads and building evidence. Sometimes, you get your perp quick, sometimes later. And sometimes, not at all."

"You don't have to tell me that, John. 'Not at all' won't work here."

Anderson rose from his chair and stood over his boss'

desk. "I'll have something soon."

The captain raised his bushy eyebrows and looked off to the side. "You're so full of it. But I've been through this with you before, and you always seem to land on your feet. I can hold the governor's office off for five, six months max." The captain leaned back. "Get it done or for all I care you can take a long leave of absence."

Anderson worked late that evening. At ten-thirty, one of his detectives interrupted him. "A bunch of us are going over to Shiners for a couple of beers. Like to join us?"

Closing his laptop, he stretched and yawned. "Think I'll take a rain check. I'm tired. Besides, I need to go on home and check in on Allison."

"Come on, John, we haven't seen you at the watering hole for months. Give your folks a call."

Anderson phoned his stepmother who encouraged him to go and reassured him that his little girl was already in bed. He left everything on his desk and drove the few blocks to the Texas Shiner Pub. Several small copper and stainless steel brew kettles lined the wall behind the bar. The smoke haze and aroma of brewing malt wafted on the conditioned air. A jukebox in the corner belted out 'Boot-Scoot'n Boogey,' and several couples danced around the small parquet floor.

He and his detective sat at the bar and downed a beer. After a half-hour, Kelly Moran, a petite sergeant from central booking, sauntered up. "Hey, Anderson. Long time no see. Want to dance?"

He turned. "No, thanks. Not now."

She smiled and sat down next to him.

Her femininity unexpectedly aroused him. "How about a beer?"

"A Shiner Bock will do fine."

Before long, 'Love me tender, love me true, never let me go,' played from the jukebox. She looked into his eyes. "How about now?"

"I don't know. It's been a long—"

She cut him off and laid her arm across his shoulder. "You're just way too serious. Don't you know there's more to life than the precinct? All work and no play makes John a dull boy."

He smiled, stood, and led her to the dance floor. For the first few steps, he held her loosely, but soon pulled her closer. They were the only two on the floor. He shut his eyes and breathed her perfume. She'd made him smile, and it was a long time since he'd smiled.

But anything could happen. After all, Elvis was in the house.

He took her out to dinner the following week, then the next and the next. Pretty soon, the budding relationship was the talk of the department. While the love was great, she impressed him with the way she integrated herself into his family.

She even got him to go to church with her every Sunday. Kelly's relationship with his daughter pleased him the most. At eleven, Allison needed the companionship of a woman she could relate to, talk to, and ask the girly questions that always embarrassed him.

The sky seemed bluer, and he exploded with happiness. Her care and attention brought back his love of life. Everything would be perfect if only he could crack the Hamilton case. Two months had passed since his captain's threat without any major breaks.

Nonetheless, he continued to investigate. Mark Allen, his FBI friend up in Dallas, confirmed the bureau and DEA had maintained surveillance on Austin's Mexican Mafia as a part of another operation going on at the time of the senator's death. None of the slime bags were anywhere near Hamilton or his apartment that night.

But it still nagged at him that the Mafia had posted a lookout on Bentsen Russell. It reverberated in his head like a beating drum. Shaking down Gomez and his boss revealed only that they had slipped the Secretary an envelope.

Both denied knowledge of the contents and claimed they were errand boys for José Perez, a higher echelon Mafia figure from Guadalajara. Said he threatened their lives if they opened it. What did they care, anyway?

He needed to question the Secretary of State, but the elusive man hid well behind the cloak of his federal office. No matter how hard he tried, Russell's legion of aides and lawyers prevented Anderson from getting anywhere close.

Finally, after several months, he caught a break. One of his law enforcement friends associated with the Texas Rangers and Department of Public Safety worked a special detail for Governor Ronald Phillips, who replaced Lovett. He arranged a meeting at a small, out of the way restaurant in the hills just outside of Austin.

Anderson took a sip of his beer. "Been trying to see Secretary Russell to ask him a few questions about the Hamilton case, but I think he's avoiding me. I can't get through his aides and front office."

The governor bit into a rib. "I find that a bit ridiculous."

"Well, so do I." Though Anderson had barely touched his steak, he pushed his plate away. "You see, sir, we have proof of contact between a Mexican Mafia messenger and the Secretary."

"What? You can't be serious. Bentsen Russell is as honest a man as you'd ever find. He's clean. Why, there's never even been a hint of a scandal connected to him."

"I'm not implying that he did anything wrong, just saying that the contact occurred. May be a tie to Senator Hamilton's murder. We need to ask him a few questions."

The governor combed his fingers through his graying hair. "And if I don't help?"

Anderson pondered the situation. "I'll give you what we have." In hushed tones, he related the funeral incident. "I'd sure hate for it to leak, but if I can talk to him, maybe we can keep it all in the family."

The state's chief executive tossed a rib down, wiped his chin then leaned in. "I want your promise. No leaks?"

"None. You have my word."

"Then I'll see what I can do."

Two weeks later, he received an invitation to Washington for an interview with Secretary of State Bentsen Russell.

American Airlines Flight 82 descended above the Potomac and touched down ten minutes early at Washington's Reagan Airport. After a short cab ride, Anderson sat in Russell's office at the State Department.

He shook Anderson's hand. "I assume you already know the rules."

Anderson nodded.

The secretary motioned to a distinguished looking, well-dressed gentleman to his right. "My personal attorney, Peter Ratigan." He then indicated the pale and thin younger man on his left. "This here's William McCormick, an aide." The latter looked barely out of college.

With the lawyer and aide acting in the roles of protector and intimidator, a straightforward approach would be difficult. Anderson scratched his head. "We have a problem, Mr. Secretary. I know you held a great admiration for Senator Hamilton."

"Of course. Besides him being my protégé, we were personal friends. Often helped each other politically."
Removing a small notebook from his inside pocket, he fumbled through it until he came to a well-scribbled page.

"Let's see. Says here." He paused. "Shoot, can't even read my own handwriting."

Russell smiled at his confusion. "Perhaps you should have been a doctor." The others in the room forced a laugh.

"Oh, yeah. Got it now. Do you know anything about a couple of guys named Juan Gomez or Jose Perez?"

"No. Can't say I do." He turned and winked at the aide. "Gomez and Perez are pretty common names in Texas." McCormick chuckled, and Russell grinned like the Cheshire cat.

"Yes, that's true." Anderson cleared his throat. "But these two have Mexican drug connections."

"Didn't know this was a DEA investigation."

"It isn't, but then again with your contacts, you might know of them." Anderson caught him in a lie and now waited to drop the other shoe, but still used caution.

"We're a bit concerned for your safety, Mr. Secretary. Gomez was seen following you at Hamilton's funeral. You might remember, he bumped into your wife."

"Someone bumping into his wife hardly warrants your concern for the secretary's safety." Ratigan shut a notebook as if to indicate the end of the meeting.

But Anderson ignored him and stared straight at Russell. "We questioned Gomez. Claimed he stuffed an envelope into your coat pocket."

The old politician's demeanor changed, and his facial expression tilted from smug to concerned. "Why, the man must be demented. I never received any envelope at the funeral. Besides, if organized crime got close enough to plant something on me, I'd turn it right over to the proper authorities."

After writing a note on his small pad, Anderson leaned back.

The young aide walked around in front of him and pointed to the door with his hand. "I'm sorry, the secretary has pressing international business, and I for one have had enough of this nonsense."

"Not nonsense," Anderson snapped. "Oh, I can see where a murder investigation may seem trivial to y'all with the world problems you solve." He stood. "Just one more thing, and then I'm fixin' to leave. I don't get it. The Mexicans follow you and slip you an envelope that you don't have. And, your IRS tax records indicate you've made more than a few sizable donations to the same Guadalajara charity for almost thirty years."

The secretary's face reddened. "My family contributes more than a million dollars a year to charities. Do you think I'm aware of each and every one?"

"Glad y'all are charitable folks, Mr. Secretary, but my people traced the money. Doesn't go to Mexico at all, but rather into an offshore account at a Grand Cayman bank. Can't quite piece it all together. Then again, maybe it's nothing."

Before his attorney could stop him, Russell rose. He shouted, and his hands flailed in the air. "Where do you come off digging into my tax records and personal business? Who the devil broke the law to give you that information?"

Anderson remained expressionless. "Well, tell you what. I have a few friends in low places. Every now and then, they slip me a tip or two."

Ratigan glared at Russell and then pointed to the door. "We're done here, detective."

Anderson flashed a military salute at the three stunned men, executed an about face and exited.

With no posted letter to trace, he had the word of criminals versus a respected and beloved politician. Who could trust either? If any money changed hands, it was accomplished with a great deal of discretion. The same sum deposited in the offshore bank was laundered back to Mexico and disappeared there.

All the way home, Anderson pondered every detail of Hamilton's death, from the time Cain and Monica left him passed out on his bed to how Russell's connection to the Mafia fit in. Cain called regularly, and as requested, reported his whereabouts.

Tracking him was not too difficult anyway. His interludes with Monica often caught the attention of the press from newspapers to a feature story in *Texas Monthly*.

Anderson still believed a professional hit man murdered the senator. He pursued leads pertaining to the drug cartel and, at the same time, kept an eye on the Fort Worth entrepreneur. He pondered a thought. If they would only strike again, maybe he could pull some loose ends together.

12 The Sunshine State

Jackson Freed. I know all about that slimy hotshot shyster all the way back to his college days. The crap he pulled on Eduardo Menendez is probably only a distant memory.

The kid messed up a little bit, but Freed completely destroyed the boy. Most of the guys kind of liked the Menendez kid except for Freed. He kept most of the brothers well supplied with drugs. And talk about good-looking chicks. He attracted them to the house like flies with his money and fancy sports cars.

Freed was jealous. All those good-looking chicks really grated on him. That's why he did his best to get Eduardo thrown out. Finally got enough votes to blackball him for moral reasons. Took it upon himself to deliver the news in person.

The kid tried to kill himself the next day.

Can you imagine that? For moral reasons? What a joke. Freed drank like a fish, smoked pot, messed with some cocaine and chased anyone in sight wearing a skirt. He cheated his way through law school. Don't know how he did it, but he had the answers to the tests before-hand.

A real evil type. And he's never changed. Now he works to get criminals off even when he knows they're guilty of the worst types of crimes.

Hey, even got some of my people off recently.

*   *   *   *   *

A few days after sending Steve Shelton back to Guadalajara, Jackson helped Hadassah into the cockpit of his twin-engine Cessna at Fort Worth's Meacham International Airport. He took off into a clear blue sky.

After stopping for fuel in Mississippi, he flew across the Gulf until warm waters crashing onto the beaches of west Florida came into view. The terrain soon changed. The Everglades spread below, an enormous flat swamp-land supporting a vast shallow river of grass with an occasional oasis of trees and shrubs.

He poured Hadassah a cup of coffee from a thermos, leaned closer, and kissed her. "We'll be there pretty soon. I want you to stay away from the people I'm working with. No socializing."

She raised her eyebrows. "That bad?"

"Mafia types. Don't trust them even if they are

lawyers. Gotta watch out they don't stab you in the back."

He banked southeast. By three-thirty, the outer reaches of the southwest portion of Dade County, Florida, appeared in the distance. He pushed his yoke forward and descended into Miami. "Tamiami tower, Cessna N-four, one, five, three, requesting landing instructions and clearance for runway twenty-three right/nine left."

"Cessna, Tamiami tower. Welcome to Miami. You're clear for a landing at that designated runway. Wind's south at two knots, temperature seventy-eight degrees Fahrenheit. Land and approach from west to east."

"Roger that, Tamiami tower." He flew alongside the airport, swung south, then banked east. He positioned his aircraft into a graceful final descent and glided smoothly onto the runway. After another two thousand feet, he spotted Oro Express, a small facility that looked in poor repair.

Several aircraft service personnel fueled and loaded boxes onto a variety of aircraft outside the terminal building. As Jackson and Haddie exited the Cessna, a small man with a fluffy handlebar moustache greeted them.

"Señor Freed, I presume."

He nodded.

"Hope you had a good trip. Your limousine awaits around front."

Vertical metal bars fortified the company's old structure on one side and steel reinforced electronic doors protected the flight operations section. Sitting at the front entrance, a lone security man with an Uzi scrutinized each customer.

At the limo, the chauffeur, a well-built man in his thirties, opened the rear door and invited them in. "First time in Miami?"

"For her. I come from time to time."

"If you need anything during your stay, entertainment, gambling, nightclubs, restaurants, what you want, I got. Just ask and, poof, I get it for you. I da man. Limo's yours for the entire stay. Got a card with my cell number. Give it to you when I drop you off at the hotel. Call me anytime."

"What's your name?" Haddie asked.

The limo driver smiled, revealing two missing front teeth. "Eddie, ma'am. Eddie Rogers."

"Have you lived here a long time?"

He adjusted his rearview mirror. "Yes, ma'am. My folks come down here from the big Chi when I was seven. You come down here for business or pleasure?"

Jackson spoke up, a bit irritated with the chauffeur's incessant questions. "Business. I'm an attorney."

"What kind of case you working on?"

"How long it will take us to get to the hotel?"

"'Bout forty-five minutes."

Jackson gazed at the half-closed window between him and the driver. "Does this thing close all the way?"

"Yeah."

"Good, then close it."

Soon, they left the expressway and drove through downtown. Just south of where the Miami River meets Biscayne Bay, the limo pulled into the driveway of the Hotel Intercontinental Miami, a wide tan marble building that rose thirty-four stories into an azure blue sky.

Jackson waited behind another guest at the reception desk who engaged in a brief animated exchange in Spanish with the clerk. Jackson replaced the dissatisfied customer and took off his Stetson and introduced himself. It took only seven minutes to get him and Haddie to the penthouse suite on the thirty-second floor overlooking the bay. And all on International Aviation's dime.

Warm pink and red hues from the sun mirrored on the bay. Darkness began to consume the heavens as the sun fell beneath the western horizon. Then the city lights illuminated the deep blue water with shimmering blushes of neon.

"Quite a view."

She looked into his eyes. "Really takes your breath away."

He stayed with her on the balcony until the last bit of daylight faded then retrieved the manila envelope left for him at the front desk. In it, he found a few copies of legal documents and a letter.

Dear Mr. Freed,

Welcome to Miami. I trust your accommodations are satisfactory. Enclosed you will find some materials pertinent to the Suarez case in summary format. We have more extensive files at our offices at 2608 Flagler Street, Suite 702. We have called a meeting at our offices for nine-thirty tomorrow morning to brief you on the case in greater detail.

Sincerely,
Donald Morgan, Attorney at Law

He sorted through the remainder of the packet, scanned background information concerning Doctor Suarez and also references to several trials that addressed tangential issues not related to the Suarez case. To his astonishment, the documents failed to cite the United States vs. Robales.

After dinner, Jackson called Eddie and arranged a nine o'clock pickup for the next morning. Exhausted from the long journey, he fell asleep in Hadassah's arms. At straight up eight, the jangling telephone awakened him. Half asleep, he reached out and picked up the receiver.

"Yes."

A computerized voice answered. "Good morning, Mr. Freed. Eight o'clock, time to rise and shine. Skies are clear and seventy-eight degrees outside. Have a nice day."

Just before leaving, he placed a gentle kiss on Haddie's forehead. Smiling, she stirred a bit and cuddled into the sheets. She snuggled into a comfortable position with her eyes partially open. "Where you going, Jackson?"

"I'm due at the Miami attorney's office in a little while. I left my American Express and Visa cards on the dining-room table, but don't go out there and buy up half of Miami."

"When will I see you?"

"Maybe around three or four. He closed the bedroom door and left.

13 Suspect

The elevator opened into the waiting room of Morgan, Morgan, and Klein's office decorated in dark hues, tufted maroon leather chairs, and dimlit portraits of what were most likely dead partners. Jackson walked up to the receptionist's desk. A blonde with black roots, big boobs, and a skimpy tight dress looked up.

"Hello. I'm Jackson Freed. I have an appointment with Mr. Donald Morgan."

She pressed a button on the office intercom. "Mistah Morgan, a Mistah Freed here to see yah." She nodded. "Right this way, sir." The faux blonde smiled as she opened the interior office door. He wondered which of the lawyers she slept with.

The partners sat around a large cherry wood table. Donald Morgan, a slender, gray-haired man in his early to mid seventies and the obvious leader of the pack, sat at the head of the conference table. He introduced himself and the others.

Jackson took mental notes.

Raymond Klein, the youngest of the three, had an olive complexion and tanned skin drawn tight from too much sun exposure. He wore a conservative dark charcoal suit, white-on-white striped dress shirt, blue tie, and a black skullcap that covered his thinning hair.

Alan Morgan, a much heavier man than his older brother, sat at the farthest end of the long table and puffed away on a Cuban cigar whose fumes saturated and fouled the air.

Donald signaled the receptionist to leave. "May I assume that you got the package we left at the hotel."

Jackson flipped the manila envelope on the table. "Yes, sir, you sure may. Picked it up when we checked in."

The elder Morgan leaned over the table and gestured with his hands. "Then you know we've got our work cut out for us."

"I understand that. Give me our timelines on an arraignment hearing and the pertinent matters."

Klein rose. "The arraignment is scheduled for day after tomorrow. I, for one, don't think that gives us adequate time to prepare our case with a new attorney coming on the scene. We can ask for a continuance based on the fact that you just arrived yesterday and need more time to review all the necessary documents."

He glared at Klein. "We have legal precedent from a

United States Appellate Court hearing in California. I figure the court will drop all of the charges against our client at the arraignment hearing. We won't need a continuance."

Alan Morgan leaned over the table, pulled a large ashtray toward him and pushed the butt of his cigar hard in the glass until it stopped smoking. "Not that simple. The United States Attorney for South Florida is trying the case herself. On top of that, they've assigned a senior judge instead of a magistrate to hear the proceedings at the arraignment level. Most unusual indeed, and frankly, I think the government has something up their collective sleeves."

Jackson shook his head. "Gentlemen, Perez hired me as the lead attorney in this case. That makes it my call. No continuance. We go to court day after tomorrow. Besides, I'm your secret weapon."

The three partners exchanged glances.

"I'll present for the defense at the hearing. I need papers to gain admission to the Air Force base in order to interview Doctor Suarez. Are those available now?"

Klein fumbled through a large folder, found the necessary documents, and handed them over.

Jackson scanned the pages then placed them in his briefcase. "I already know the United States Attorney for South Florida, Margareth Cornish. I've faced her and beaten her ass in three previous trials. Tell me more about our judge."

"Stanley Abramowitz. Almost always sides with the

feds. Very biased against our type of client. Old, cranky, and hard to deal with."

Jackson grinned. "Gentlemen, sounds like a challenge."

The elder Morgan rose from the table. "We have comprehensive background files on the Suarez case and related material here in the office. Feel free to review then consult with any of us at any time."

"Thank you for your invitation. However, first I want to drive to Homestead and interview our client."

An hour later, Eddie's limo pulled up to the security booth at the military base. A guard in Air Force blues, white gloves and a shiny silver buckle signaled them to stop. The sergeant peered through the half-open window. "Who's the passenger?"

"Jackson Freed, a lawyer from Texas. He's come to see a prisoner you're holding on the base. A Mexican guy named Suarez."

He pointed to a vacant parking area near the security booth. "Pull in and park your vehicle, please. I'll have to contact my superior."

The sergeant finished his call and walked to the Cadillac. "I need both of you out of the car. Mr. Freed, may I please see your papers?"

Jackson dug into his briefcase, removed the folder containing the appropriate credentials and handed them to the non-commissioned officer.

The man inspected each page in a slow, methodical manner. "Do you have any other kind of identification?"

Jackson pulled his wallet out and removed his driver's license, voter's registration and social security card, then handed them over.

Reading each ID, he asked Jackson to repeat his social security number, voting district and driver's license number. Only then did he return them. "I've been instructed to search your briefcase and the limousine."

Jackson handed over the leather satchel.

The guy looked through the materials then explored every corner of the limo, even felt about the seams in the trunk, pulled back loose matting, opened the tire well and removed the spare.

He faced Jackson. "Suarez is being held near the brig in barracks five-zero-four-A." He then assumed a ramrod straight position, gave a brisk salute, and waved them through.

The security officer at the barracks' entrance reviewed Jackson's papers again and instructed him to wait. After a few minutes, a guard led Suarez, handcuffed and attired in drab blue military fatigues, through the door. The guard then moved to the back of the room and sat down.

"I'll talk to my client alone." Jackson pointed to the exit. "The law allows me to talk to him privately without you present."

"Very well, sir. Ring the buzzer in the middle of the table when you finish."

Sitting on a small wooden chair across the table from the Mexican doctor, Jackson removed a file, legal notebook, and an electronic pad from his briefcase. "I'm Jackson Freed. Mr. Perez hired me to lead your legal defense. Do you speak English?"

"Yes. I completed much of my medical training in the states."

Jackson wrote on his electronic notepad. 'Watch what you say, never know who's listening' then slid it toward Suarez together with the stylus. He studied his client a moment. Suarez appeared almost too calm and relaxed. "They treating you okay, Doc?"

"Yes, the food is very good, and I have a private bath with a Jacuzzi."

He smiled. At least Suarez had some humor under duress. "How did you get into this mess?"

The Mexican man rested his head in his hands and rubbed his forehead. "I was forced into it at both ends."

"But you carried Mr. Menendez's identification papers. Seems to me that you volunteered to take your friend's place. And that, my good doctor, constitutes conspiracy."

Suarez took a deep breath. "Please, sir, let me share my background. Pablo Menendez and I were born into very poor families and lived next door to each other in a Guadalajara slum. Times were very bad. Our families became close to survive.

"When I turned five, a man killed my father in a local bar. Pablo's father took my mother and me into his home and supported us. We became like brothers, so much so, that people thought his father was mine."

Suarez leaned on the table and looked down. "At fifteen, Pablo went to work for a Mafia gang that robbed, murdered, dealt in drugs, and sold protection. He was very good at what he did and quickly moved up their ladder to a high-ranking position.

"That wasn't my lifestyle or ambition. I wanted to become a doctor so that I could help people. Pablo supported me throughout my schooling. Believe me. That took a great deal of money. Although we differed greatly, our relationship grew deeper."

Suarez sat more upright and pulled his hand across his face in one slow, sweeping motion. "When Pablo pulled his own group together, he asked me to join. I declined. Physicians in Mexico, unlike in the States, make precious little money and often have trouble making ends meet. So his offer tempted me.

"Pablo continued to aid me by referring family members, friends, people from his organization, politicians, anyone he owned or influenced. I will tell you, I had many patients then.

"Out of love and respect for our friendship and families, he included me in a few of his legitimate businesses as well. I'm of course his personal physician, and advise him on friends, women, and an occasional business matter.

"That's about where it stopped until—" Suarez paused. He closed his eyes, rubbed the side of his nose and sighed, " —until that time when he called me at two o'clock in the morning to ask about his mother."

Jackson wrote a note on his electronic pad. "What made things change?"

"Someone took Pablo's mother to the hospital by ambulance. I knew nothing about it. He suspected an assassination attempt. Maybe he thought it involved me. I don't know. He wanted me to take his place and go to the hospital instead of him. At first, I refused."

Suarez lowered his head. "Then for the first time since I knew him, he threatened me. One does not take a threat from Pablo Menendez lightly. When he tells you it is not in the best interest of your health to refuse, it means that if you don't go along, he'll kill you.

"So as you can see, Mr. Freed, I had no choice. My survival depended on playing along with his mistaken identity plan."

Jackson adjusted his chair. "And that was the night you were kidnapped?"

"Yes. I left his house in his car, wore one of his suits, and carried his ID. It was almost impossible for a stranger to tell us apart."

Jackson rubbed the side of his nose. "When did the arresting agents know they had the wrong person?"

"At first, everything was crazy. Gunfire, shouting, trucks, and helicopters. No one realized it then."

"So they thought they had the right guy?"

"In the beginning, yes. When they got me on the plane to fly back to the States, they declared I was Pablo and began to quote some statement about my rights. I, of course, corrected them and told them they kidnapped the wrong person. The one in charge made me drop my slacks then looked at my buttocks for an identifying mark.

"That's when they realized I spoke the truth, but it didn't change their intentions. They brought me to this place and have held me since."

Did they go over your rights again after they discovered who you really were? Jackson scribbled this sentence on the electronic pad and passed it and an accompanying stylus to the doctor.

He wrote *no, never again.*

Jackson reclaimed the equipment and erased the answer immediately. "Have they interrogated you?"

"All the time, and keep me awake by playing blaring music that stops at three-thirty a.m. sharp every day. Otherwise, everything's fine."

"Did they inform you that you had the right not to answer questions without an attorney present?"

Suarez shook his head.

"Were you able to give the investigators any of the information they sought?"

"Not much. I know very little about Pablo's drug business. My inquisitors probably know much more about his operations than I do."

"Your arraignment is scheduled for day after tomorrow. We'll bring you a conservative suit and tie. The government will charge you with conspiracy in the murder of Ricardo Hernandez, a United States DEA operative killed in Mexico."

Suarez's face grew very taut. "I know nothing of this."

"I believe you. We'll plead your innocence."

At three o'clock, Eddie drove under the archway of Homestead Air Force Base. Its sign read: "The Two Hundred and Twenty-Fourth Tactical Air Command. For Freedom and Liberty."

14 Priorities

Arriving at the Intercontinental forty-five minutes later, Jackson found Haddie sprawled across the bed. Shopping bags overflowed with clothes, shoes, scarves and handbags. Her purchases littered the room.

She stretched, rose and kissed him. "Everything go alright?"

He looked at her loot and grinned. "Should have known better than to let you loose with those cards. Looks like you bought half of Miami, after all."

She laughed. "As a matter of fact, I found this nice little shopping center on the waterfront just a few blocks from the hotel. Wonderful little boutiques, restaurants, shops, shops, and more shops. Did all my damage there."

"At least you weren't bored while I sweated away. Let me see what you got."

Haddie unpacked her bounty, including a designer watch for Jackson. He hugged her, and they fell onto the bed amidst plastic bags and new garments.

"Jack? Jack!" she protested, then lost her voice to a prolonged kiss.

He pulled his fingers through her long, red hair. "Good G-d, Haddie, I love you."

"I love you, too," she replied between shortened breaths. They dozed off in each other's arms.

He awoke relaxed and confident. Jackson looked forward to the impending legal battle. He believed that Donald Morgan was the most knowledgeable and experienced of the Miami legal team and picked him to sit as his second chair for the trial.

Just before the arraignment, he and the elder Morgan met in a cramped antechamber at the Federal Courthouse.

At nine sharp, he entered the courtroom of the United States District Court for Southern Florida. A noisy air-conditioning system provided little relief from the South Atlantic heat and humidity. The room smelled mildewed and damp, and the air stagnant.

As always, Jackson wore his white Stetson.

At a little after the hour, the prosecution team took their places led by Margareth Cornish, a large woman in her late forties who dwarfed most of her counterparts.

Jackson walked to his opponents' table until he stood over the seated six-foot-one prosecutor. She gazed up, her prominent cheekbones shadowing acne-pocked skin.

"Well, as I live and breathe, if it's not my old nemesis Jackson Freed. Don't you ever take that silly hat off? You're in Florida for heaven's sake, not Texas."

"Only for the judge."

"A gentleman till the end."

"Nice to see you. Still the consummate lady. You're the only woman in the world I know who can make business proper look like hell." He smiled just enough to annoy her, turned his back and sauntered back to the defense table.

Morgan finished a doodle on his legal pad then looked up. "What was that all about?"

"Intimidation. She's a lousy loser."

The bailiff escorted Doctor Suarez to his seat.

After what seemed like an eternity, Senior Judge Stanley Abramowitz stormed in from his chambers with the face of a bulldog. Red fleshy cheeks extended down below his jawbone. Creases of skin hung loosely from his neck, and stiff strands of hair stood up from his ears. His voice was deep, stern, and forceful.

"Miss Cornish and Mr. Freed, this is an arraignment hearing, so I do not expect nor will I tolerate any theatrics. Do you both understand?"

"Yes, your honor."

"Miss Cornish, you may proceed."

She rose from the prosecution table. "Your honor, in the case of The United States versus Doctor Humberto Suarez, the people charge Doctor Suarez with conspiracy in the murder of United States Drug Enforcement

Agent Ricardo Hernandez."

Suarez sat stone-faced at the defense table.

"Mr. Freed, how say you, and how does your client plead?" Abramowitz's gaze fell on Jackson like a boulder.

He stood and walked up to the defense lectern. "Your honor, this entire arraignment hearing is a sham."

Margareth Cornish jumped up from her seat. "I object. It's time to enter a plea, not make an opening statement."

"Overruled. Mr. Freed, I'll give you a little leeway for now, but this better lead to something."

"Thank you, your honor. I will take no more than five minutes of the court's time. First of all, Doctor Suarez is a Mexican national and a prominent physician. While he has nothing to do with drugs or drug trafficking, he does have the misfortune of being the boyhood friend of the infamous Mexican drug lord Pablo Menendez.

"The two men have a great resemblance. However, that does make him a conspirator in the murder of Ricardo Hernandez."

Rising again from the prosecution table, Margareth leaned on the desk. "Your honor, I must object. Again, this is an opening statement. We're gathered this morning to charge the defendant and hear how he pleads."

"Miss Cornish, you are overruled. Please sit down."

Slamming a legal pad on the table, she sank into her seat.

Jackson figured it should be over in a matter of

minutes. He moved closer to the judge.

"I would like to point out, your honor, a case of the United States versus Robales, the Federal Appellate Court in California ruled that Doctor Robales be returned to Mexico because he was a Mexican national illegally arrested in that country by U.S. Drug Enforcement Agents.

"This overturned a conviction by a lower court. Furthermore, your honor, my client was never properly read his Miranda rights."

The judge's forehead furrowed, and his mouth twisted into a frown. "Before you go any further, you two approach."

Jackson stood beside Cornish in front of the elderly jurist. "What about Mr. Freed's accusations relative to Miranda?"

"It's the first I've heard of it, and I don't believe he's correct, your honor. As far as I know, the arresting officers certainly did read him his rights."

Jackson shook his head. "Caught with your panties down, Margareth. Why don't you admit it?"

The judge's eyes narrowed, and he glared. "That will be quite enough, Mr. Freed. I don't know what they let you get away with in Texas, but in my court, that remark is not acceptable."

"I sincerely apologize to the federal prosecutor and his honor. I was out of line."

"I want both of you in my chambers. Right now!" Abramowitz stood up and led the way to his small office behind the courtroom. Jackson, Morgan, Cornish and her associates followed.

The judge straightened a stack of papers on his desk. "Would someone mind telling me what is going on here?"

Jackson cleared his throat. "Your honor, the DEA picked up the wrong man and couldn't come to grips with it, even though they knew the truth a short time after the arrest. They were after Pablo Menendez, but they got Suarez by mistake."

The judge motioned toward the prosecution team. "What about that, Miss Cornish?"

She tapped the table a couple of times with a pencil and leaned forward. "Well, the man had all of Menendez's identification papers on his person."

Jackson interrupted. "Yes, she's right about that, but he carried all those papers under duress."

Abramowitz swiveled in his chair until he faced the defense team. "Do you know that for a fact?"

"Yes, sir, and we can prove it."

Cornish threw her hands in the air. "But, judge, he's a member of the Menendez crime family, and that makes him a co-conspirator."

"The devil it does. Having an acquaintance and a similar appearance does not make you a co-conspirator to murder. It appears you've made too many leaps of faith in your case, Margareth."

The judge, his face flushed, peered at them with gray eyes glaring from deep, darkened sockets. "Enough.

What about your Miranda claims, Mr. Freed?"

"When they kidnapped Dr. Suarez, the agents put him on a C-130 and flew him to Miami. During the flight, they began reading Pablo Menendez his rights, but Doctor Suarez interrupted them and informed them that they had the wrong man.

"The DEA forced him to disrobe. The lead agent noticed that an identifying tattoo on the suspect's buttocks was missing and realized the terrible truth. At that point, they had nothing to charge my client with. The arresting officers never restated a Miranda to Suarez, nor did they accuse him of any other crime. He's been held for two weeks in detention at Homestead Air Force Base without the benefit of any formal charges."

His old adversary shrugged. "Come on now, Jackson. That's a technicality, and you know it."

"Tell that to my client."

The jurist rose and leaned over his table. "It's a technicality nonetheless. Let's go back into the courtroom."

Jackson and the other attorneys slowly filed back followed by the judge who, once behind his bench, rapped his gavel.

"I'll take our discussion under advisement for forty-eight hours. At that time, I'll make a decision relative to the allegations."

Jackson loosened his tie. "You honor, may my client be dismissed from detention?"

Cornish jumped to her feet. "Your honor, the defendant is a large stockholder in American International

Aviation. The company has planes based in Miami, and the government's fear of flight is very real."

"Your remarks are well taken. The court will not permit bail nor freedom from confinement." Abramowitz began to rise.

"Hang on there a minute, your honor. My client's not charged with any crime. How can you legally hold him?"

"Mr. Freed, you are trying the court's patience. I am ancient and crabby, and I certainly wouldn't want you to press your luck. Hope we understand each other, counselor."

Jackson nodded.

"I remand the prisoner to the custody of the federal marshals for transportation to Homestead Air Force Base where he will be held for the next forty-eight hours. When we reconvene, I will clear up this matter one way or the other."

Jackson put his arm around Suarez's shoulders and reassured him. "You'll be a free man day after tomorrow. Don't do anything foolish that might jeopardize your release."

The bailiff cuffed Suarez and handed him over to three federal marshals. While she gathered her things, Cornish glared at Jackson, but did not exchange any words.

Spending the next morning at Morgan, Morgan, and Klein, Jackson planned contingencies in case Abramowitz did not release Suarez. He also prepared for a messy preliminary hearing. Cornish had looked as though she was taking the gloves off as Jackson left the courtroom.

Either option would keep him in Miami longer than he had anticipated, and that disturbed him. Separation from his son for more than a few days made him very uncomfortable. If the trial lagged, he decided he'd fly Robbie and Mrs. Herrin to Miami.

As darkness approached, Eddie drove Jackson and Hadassah to Coconut Grove where they feasted on Florida stone crabs. After dinner, he strolled with her hand in hand past quaint restaurants and bars, on occasion stopping at antique shops, art galleries or sidewalk craft displays. He lingered at the bay's view awash in sailboats floating on dark, still waters.

He felt pretty good. Perhaps the Miami atmosphere soothed his usual anxiety. Whatever ruling Abramowitz made, the trial would sooner or later end in his client's favor. The pleasant stroll ended near the limo where Eddie waited. Jackson wanted to get back to the room and hold more than Haddie's hand.

The telephone was ringing when he opened the door to the suite. "Mister Freed? I'm the unit secretary with the Pediatric Intensive Care Unit at Cook Children's Medical Center. Are you the father of Robbie Freed?"

"Yes, what's this about?" Jackson sank down onto the plush sofa and tried to swallow. His heart stopped beating.

"Please hold. The doctor will be with you shortly."

Haddie moved next to him and wrapped her arm

around him. "What is it, Jackson? What's wrong?"

"Don't know just yet. It's the children's hospital back home, intensive care unit, and she wanted to know if I was Robbie's father. I'm holding for the doctor."

"Hello? Mr. Freed?"

"Yes. I'm Jackson Freed. What's going on?"

"I'm afraid your son has been involved in a very serious accident."

Jackson stared at the floor. "What happened? How bad is it?"

"He was hit by a car and sustained a closed head injury. He hasn't regained consciousness."

Jackson closed his eyes and winced. Tears rolled down his cheeks. "Will he survive?"

"There's a lot of swelling. He's on life supports. I don't know what turn his condition will take, but his injuries are very critical."

"What about his nanny?"

"I don't know. He came in alone."

"I'll get there as quick as I can, doc. Thanks."

Jackson hung up the receiver. He put his hands on Hadassah's shoulders and buried his face in her bosom, wetting her blouse with his tears.

She ran her hand through his hair and held him. "Oh my G-d, Jack. What's going on?"

"We need to get back. A car hit Robbie. The doctor says he might not make it."

He called the elder Morgan. Donald was up in years and from the sound of his voice, Jackson had awakened him. "For Pete's sake, it's ten-forty. Didn't your mother ever teach you not to call people after nine?"

"I'm sorry, but my boy's in intensive care. Had a bad accident. I'm leaving for Fort Worth tonight."

The elderly attorney fumbled the phone. "But Freed, we're scheduled in court in the morning. I'm sorry to hear your bad news, but sounds like he's in good hands. Can't you leave after this case is wrapped up?"

"My kid comes first. Doc says he might die."

"Our client needs both of us to defend him if Abramowitz's decision goes down bad. I can handle it myself, but Perez specifically wants you there. He won't like this one little bit."

Jackson's bowels growled. "If you don't think you can handle it without me, then get a continuance. I'll take the case over when I get back."

"I'm telling you, it'll make Perez mad, and you really don't want to do that."

"I don't care if he puts me in cement boots, you'll have to handle the judge. I'm leaving tonight. End of conversation!" He slammed down the phone, chipping off a small piece of plastic from the receiver.

He called Oro Express at Tamiami Airport and instructed the mechanic on duty to get his plane flight-ready as quickly as possible.

"No problem, Mr. Freed. We'll get you taken care of within an hour," the night foreman reassured him.

Eddie dropped him and Haddie off at the airport an hour and a half later. Jackson rewarded him for his service with five crisp one hundred-dollar bills. He ordered his fuel tanks capped off to avoid a refueling stop. Anxious and fatigued, he took extra time going over his checklist.

He switched on his ignition. At first, the engines sputtered, but soon the aircraft sprung to life. The tower closed at midnight, but the well-lit field posed no hazard.

Thick hot air added to the heavy stillness of both the night and his heart. Not one hint of wind pierced the humidity. Small droplets of water accumulated on the leading edges of the Cessna.

Jackson taxied onto runway twenty-seven right/nine left and positioned his plane to the west thirty-five hundred feet from his point of liftoff. Spotlights from a nearby medical research facility silhouetted a large clump of twelve-foot high saw grass and thick brush at the end of the runway.

A westward takeoff would put him out over the Everglades heading home. He brought the plane to a standstill, gunned the engines to full throttle and released the brakes. The craft surged forward. It raced down the runway.

Jackson rotated the nose upward and began to climb into the black night sky. At two hundred and fifty feet, he noticed a bright light with a trailing tail coming from the thick saw grass and bushes to his left.

Fireworks?

The rounded light with a comet's tail continued to weave its way directly toward him. All of a sudden the small plane shuddered.

Overloaded with fuel, the aircraft burst into a ball of fire that trajected upward and illuminated the evening sky. In a shower of death, each piece by minute piece of the Cessna and human remains spiraled back to the asphalt pavement at the end of twenty-seven right/nine left. Charred heaps of burning rubble littered the runway.

15 Tequila Oro

A loud banging on his door startled Steve Shelton awake. Hoping whoever it was would go away, he stirred a little, but denied full consciousness. The intrusive knocking continued. And after a little while longer, he shook off the beer and tequila grog.

Retrieving his Glock from beneath his pillow, he hurried to the door, cracked it, and stared into the dimlit patio. A young Mexican boy moved back a few inches. "Señor Shelton?"

"Yeah. What do you want?"

"Mr. Perez needs to see you. He said I should bring you to him right now."

Steve yawned. "At three o'clock in the morning? He's crazy. Tell him he can wait until a decent hour."

The boy grimaced, and his eyelids narrowed. "No, no, no. Please, mister. I'll be beaten. Please come now. I'm sure it's muy importante." The kid thrust forward a note. "Hurry, señor, there's a car waiting." He passed the crumpled piece of paper through the opening in the door.

Through foggy vision, Steve struggled to read the writing.

> *Urgent business. Must discuss immediately. Pedro will escort you to Senor Menendez's villa.*
>
> *José Perez*

What was that supposed to mean? Well, can't be anything good this time of night. Maybe they wanted to kill him, put him out of his misery. He opened the door a bit wider. "All right, all right. I'll get dressed already."

He slipped his semiautomatic into his rear waistband, wrote a quick note to his Fort Worth office and placed it into the hotel's mail drop on his way out.

The young boy led him to a black Cadillac limousine and then melted into the darkness. Driving past the outskirts of Guadalajara, the chauffeur remained as silent as a stone statue. Across a flat plain, fewer and fewer houses cropped up, and with each ensuing mile, the landscape became nothing more than an occasional giant cactus or century plant illuminated by the moonlight.

If anyone intended foul play, Steve knew he wouldn't have a chance. He pondered options and contingency plans. His palms sweated, and his heart pounded. He hated that and reached behind his pants to wipe his hands and adjust his weapon.

Out of the tinted windows, mountains came into view, and the car climbed on a crude road. Loose gravel pelted its underbelly. The limo finally stopped. The driver flashed his headlights four times.

Huge beams from a parapet crisscrossed the automobile and almost blinded him. Then solid metal gates slid into adjoining concrete walls jutting out from the mountain. The car stopped again in front of a well-lit pink villa in the center of the compound. One might think it was broad daylight.

Steve glanced up and faced the end of a sawed-off shotgun pointing through his open window. "Get out, Gringo, and keep your hands where I can see them."

He slid across the seat, and as he exited, the hands of a greasy-haired cartel bodyguard moved across his torso.

"Hey, I'm here at Perez's request. What's this all about?"

"Give me your gun."

He raised his hands just to the side of his head. Comfortable as he could be, knowing that he carried another pistol and knife in his boots, he surrendered the weapon at his waist. Losing one out of three? Not all that bad.

The guard led him into a wood-paneled library. José Perez rose from a leather chair. "Good morning, Mr. Shelton. Welcome."

Two other men he'd never met stood at the bar. He thought one of them was the drug lord himself, Pablo Menendez. After a couple of deep breaths, he swallowed a large wad of dry spit. What did these thugs want?

The cartel leader put down his glass and shook Steve's hand. "Pablo Menendez, Mr. Shelton. I hear you've done good work on behalf of Doctor Suarez. May I offer you a drink?"

"Tequila Oro straight up."

He poured two ounces of tequila into a glass. "Please, have a seat, Mr. Shelton. We have troubling news."

He wondered what had happened and downed the liquor in one rapid swig. The pit of his stomach burned. "What news?"

Pablo's forehead wrinkled, and his lips contorted into a frown. "A missile shot down Mr. Freed's airplane as he attempted to take off from Tamiami."

"What? What are you talking about? That's crazy. The case wasn't done, was it? Jackson never leaves an unfinished case."

"Our people at the airport witnessed the incident. A fiery object headed toward his Cessna soon after takeoff, and the plane went down in many pieces. There were no survivors."

"Your people saw it or fired it?" He took a step toward Menendez. For a brief moment, everything in the room grew still as his fist cut through the air. The Mexican mobster moved to the side and ducked.

His face hardened and he glared at Steve. "I wouldn't

advise you to try that again. You're dead with a snap of my fingers."

Taking a deep breath, Steve backed off toward the bar and poured himself another drink. Beads of sweat dripped from his brow and stung his eyes. "But, it can't be true!"

"I'm afraid it is, though I wish it were not. The aircraft incinerated in midair."

Steve's bowels roared. He struggled to maintain composure. Not the time to fall apart. "But why did he leave Miami so suddenly?"

Menendez shrugged. "It seems he got word that his son was critically injured in an automobile accident."

"Robbie? Oh, no. Who's responsible?"

"We have no information as to who may have done this terrible thing. I only wish to reassure you that no member of our organization was involved. It is true that we held great admiration and respect for Mr. Freed and in no way wanted harm to befall him."

Steve's eyes looked from one Mafioso to the other. The story made no sense. They had to have something to do with the shoot down and were covering it up. Why else would they bring him there?

Whatever. He'd get whoever did it one way or another. He breathed deeply, trying to control his anger.

"How fast can I get back to Fort Worth?"

Menendez passed his fingers through his beard. "One of our jets stands ready to take you home as we speak."

Steve nodded. "May I have my gun back?"

The drug lord motioned to one his bodyguards. "Give the señor his pistole when he leaves."

As the sun began to paint the Texas sky red and orange, the cartel's Lear jet set down at DFW International Airport.

Steve deplaned at the general aviation gate at terminal Three West and called the office. Thank G-d for the best news, Robbie's condition had been upgraded from critical to serious. Looked like the boy would come off life supports in a couple of days.

Investigating on his own for a few weeks, Steve got nowhere. Rather than helping him, the Miami PD and FAA threw up barrier after barrier. Could they have been involved?

He couldn't sleep, his head ached, and stubble covered his face. This thing was eating him alive.

Then a month into what had been one dead-end after another, a law enforcement friend called to set up a meeting. Mark Allen wanted to compare notes and discuss some interesting twists and turns that might be pertinent to Jackson's case.

At two straight up the next day, Steve entered the sterile FBI offices in Dallas. The rows of dull office furniture, work cubicles, black file cabinets and flickering computer screens hadn't changed an iota since he worked there as a clerk to finance his way through college.

He and a bright young agent fresh out of the academy became best of friends. Fifteen years later, Mark had been promoted to director of the Dallas regional office.

His old friend had put on some weight over the years, but still looked to be in shape.

It took Steve half an hour to lay out what he knew. "What kind of missile brought Freed down?"

"A stinger."

"What? Where would someone get ahold of a stinger?"

The director's forehead furrowed, and he blinked his eyes hard a couple of times. "During the war, we supplied them to the Afghanistan Mujahadeen, during their fight with the old Soviet Union. At the end of that conflict, the CIA couldn't account for most of them." He shrugged.

"Hard to keep something like that out of the hands of international arms dealers. They probably sold them to third world countries including Latin American drug cartels. We have no clue as to where the one that disintegrated Freed's plane came from. Not yet, anyway.

"The idea to piece this together came from an old friend of mine. Lieutenant John Anderson's a detective in the Austin PD. He's been working the murder of a state senator. You might remember, Travis Hamilton? Died the same night he declared intentions to run for governor."

"Yeah, sure. It was in all the papers."

"Well Anderson always thought that the killer of the senator would show his hand somewhere else. When Jackson Freed was killed, I looked at things from a different perspective. His death and several of the cases we've been following here at the FBI seemed to fall into line with Anderson's theory.

"A judge named Jonathan Edwin Sherman. Everyone called him Hanging Jon for his strong verdicts against drug dealers, was assassinated five years ago in San Antonio, and his assailant was never caught.

"Perry Nicholson went on a fishing trip to a lake in a remote part of Mexico three years ago. He and his guide vanished. Never found a trace."

Steve pulled his chair closer to the desk. "How do those cases tie into Jackson and the senator?"

"All these men had one thing in common." The director raised his index finger in the air and shook it. "Only one. All were members of the Kappa Gamma Kappa fraternity at the University of Texas at Austin, class of 1970.

"And when we started running them down, we discovered there's been several other frat brothers who either died or disappeared under unusual circumstances in the last few years."

Steve frowned and scratched his sideburns. "What happened to them?"

"One had serious issues. Into the IRS for a million bucks. Went missing two years ago. Another had a scuba diving accident. One drove a car that careened out of control on a mountain road and crashed. Four apparently met their end by natural causes, except now, we're reexamining those deaths. Your boss was number eleven from this group."

"So it's an unlucky fraternity. Doesn't mean any of the deaths were connected to Jackson."

"Don't be so hardheaded. Look at the percentages." Mark poured some cold water into a glass on his desk. "Someone has a vendetta against UT's Kappa Gamma Kappa."

"Could be random."

"No." Mark shook his head. "Too much of a coincidence for me to write off."

Rising from the chair, Steve stared out the office window for a few seconds. "Assuming this Detective Anderson's suspicions are correct, it sure would take extensive resources to pull off so many assassinations. Short of a government or a drug cartel, who might have that kind of capability?"

"Good question."

Steve warmed to the idea. "So how many are left?"

"Just four." The director raised a finger as he mentioned each name. "Robert Schwartz, a Fort Worth pediatrician. Adam Cain, right here in Dallas. He's an entrepreneur and philanthropist. Rabbi Arnold Weiss, and Anthony Carr, an importer-exporter."

"We've been watching the three who live in the area, but Carr's in Hong Kong, a bit beyond my jurisdiction."

"Have you warned them?"

"It's been discussed. But we might be warning the perp." Mark rose from his chair and began to escort

Steve out of his office. "Call me if you come across anything."

16 The Short List

Anthony Carr gives me a problem, a real inner conflict. A bit pompous, but he treats people with a great deal of respect. My guys don't have much of a gripe with him, either.

Living so far away makes logistics very difficult. However, I got connections, and they can take care of business for me anywhere in the world, even China.

But why do you get rid of such a nice man? Then again, he was the driver that night in Austin. All the way up to the top. To his credit, he evidently didn't drag the poor kid into the woods. He supposedly stayed in the car and waited for the others.

Didn't vote for the blackballing of the Mexican kid, either. But then again, he didn't fight too hard against it.

I keep arguing that we should keep him alive, but my people say that wouldn't be fair to the others we wasted.

If only I could avoid killing him. I feel awful. We should really leave him alone. He's one of the good guys.

Possibly I can persuade them. Maybe not, but I'll give it my best shot.

*　*　*　*　*

Hong Kong

Anthony Carr's Lincoln stopped in front of the austere black metal and glass Iron Eagle building. He ascended to the eighth floor and arrived at his office at the far end of the facility.

The business he'd built gave him great pride. Finding non-consigned shipments arriving in Hong Kong for customers all over the world had served him well. He stopped in the office of Samantha Li King, his executive secretary, which fronted his.

He'd hired her several years ago after admiring her beautiful Eurasian appearance and being captivated by her mixture of Asian mysticism and intrinsic English ladylike politeness. She intrigued him from the start. Throw in efficiency, knowledge, and elegance and it all added up.

For the past two years, he lived with her on Lantu Island, and six months ago, bought her a five-carat diamond ring and proposed.

Samantha followed him into his work area and closed the door. He turned and winked. "Anything important I should know?"

She smiled. Her long black hair fell over one shoulder. "Usual sixes and twelves with the exception of one call."

"From whom?"

"A man name of Mark Allen. He's with the FBI, out of the Dallas office."

"Say what he wanted?"

She shrugged. "No, not really. I tried to get something out of him, but he kept reiterating that he needed to talk only with you as soon as possible about a very urgent matter."

Anthony sat behind his hand-carved Oriental desk and folded his arms. "He leave a number?"

She nodded. "Yes. Want me to ring him up for you?"

"No, I'll wait a while. I need to evaluate that transaction with the Japanese then call them first." He checked his Rolex. "We'll try Allen in an hour or two."

She smiled, "Sure," and returned to her desk. He looked out his window at the freighters and junks plying the harbor and tried to figure out what the FBI might want with him. Maybe he should go ahead and call.

An hour later, Samantha opened his door. "That FBI guy is on the phone again. Says he's about to leave his office for the evening. Should I tell him you'll call back?"

Anthony rhythmically drummed his fingers on the desk several times. "No. Put him on through."

"Agent Allen, you are quite a distance away. I've broken no laws. What's this about?" He pushed a stack of paperwork to the side. Samantha raised her eyebrows obviously wanting to know what was going on.

"Did you attend UT Austin in the nineteen-seventies and did you belong to Kappa Gamma Kappa fraternity?"

"Yes, I'd suppose that's a matter of record. What's it to you that I was at UT in 1970? That was a long time ago."

"Sir, I'll come straight to the point. I don't know how well you've kept up, but most of your fraternity brothers are dead. Only three others and you are still alive. Of those who passed on, four were murdered for sure, and many of the others expired under suspicious circumstances.

"We considered it wise to warn you. We believe that a serial killer is stalking the members of Kappa Gamma Kappa, Class of '70."

"Mr. Allen, I've had no contact with any college friends for more than twenty years. And besides, the last time I even visited the States was three years ago. At the moment, I'm fourteen hours and more than ten thousand miles west of Texas.

"Why should I be worried about an alleged serial killer on the other side of the Pacific? It's much more probable that a murderer would pick another victim on the mainland. Frankly, I'd be for warning them if you think it's necessary. The entire theory sounds rather ludicrous to me."

"Don't feel so smug for distance's sake. One of the victims disappeared outside the continental United States, and we never found him. Being in Hong Kong may not afford you any degree of safety."

"Agent Allen, I know how to take care of myself."

"But we wanted—"

"Look, Allen, I'm getting married, and we leave for our honeymoon in Hawaii right after the wedding. I've no time for this sort of nonsense. Perhaps, after we return to Hong Kong, we can discuss this matter at greater length."

"But Hawaii will put you much closer to the mainland and in greater danger. At least, let us offer protection while you're there."

"On my honeymoon? Thank you, no. I want privacy, not protection."

"But, I think—"

Anthony hung up the phone.

Two weeks later on a sunny Sunday afternoon, he and Samantha were married at Saint Thomas Protestant Cathedral. The next morning, they sat in the first class section of a Southern Pacific Airways 747-400.

Soon the jumbo-sized aircraft lumbered down Kai Tai Airport's runway that extended out onto Victoria Harbor. The big plane pointed its nose toward the sky and soon soared over the waters. It passed over the emerald colored hills of San Ki Wan, Jung and Luang Islands, edging between the bluffs and small mountains of these little projections in the South China Sea, then gained altitude and banked toward Hawaii.

Sitting in the first row, Anthony gazed about the cabin and noted only four other passengers occupied the premium section behind him.

Near the completion of dinner, a tall thin blond gentleman from the last row moved forward to the aisle seat adjacent to Anthony. He stared at the front of the cabin for a few moments and then turned to face them.

"My name is Alain Corseau. You look very much in love. Honeymooners, n'est-ce pas?"

Samantha leaned forward and smiled. "Yes, we were married yesterday."

"I would love to be going to Hawaii on vacation, but I have a business appointment in Honolulu. I represent an aviation company, and we're seeking landing rights in Oahu." The Frenchman grinned. "What is your line of work, sir?"

"Import-export out of Hong Kong."

Corseau brushed back an unruly blond lock. "Ah, then, monsieur, I know our paths have inadvertently crossed."

Anthony soon grew tired of the man's ramblings and yawned. Thankfully, the Frenchman took the hint and returned to his seat.

The blue and green 747 plowed through the air at thirty-five thousand feet. As the day faded over the Pacific, the sun began to set, painting the sky crimson and lavender. The colorful spectrum bathed Honolulu as the plane descended in its approach toward the shoreline.

The famous Diamondhead volcano stood magnificently off in the distance. Lights of the city appeared in small clusters, slowly spread along the shoreline, then marched up the green slopes of the volcano as the huge aircraft touched down.

"Excuse me, Mr. Carr." Anthony turned from pulling down Samantha's carry-on bag from the overhead compartment. The flight attendant held out a business card. "Mr. Corseau asked me to give you this."

Anthony had been pondering the blond Frenchman and his odd behavior. Now, it was obvious.

"Thank you." Anthony glanced back to the last row, but the gentleman was nowhere to be seen.

Speeding toward the hotel in a service car, he studied the card. "Alain Corseau, Executive Vice President, American International Aviation." In the corner was written "European Division, Marseilles."

17 Hawaii

Anthony and Samantha didn't leave their room the first two days then toured the Kona area on the morning of the third. Several guests told of beautiful and exciting rides over active volcanic flows. They piqued Anthony's curiosity and sense of adventure, so he booked a flight for the next evening.

Near sunset, a bright colored Gecko Airways Bell Jet Ranger landed on a helicopter pad at the hotel. The figure of a small smiling reptile in a circle was painted on the side of the orange and coral craft. When he and Samantha boarded the helicopter, the pilot motioned them to sit in the two back seats and put on the available earphones.

The copter lifted off effortlessly at a minimal angle and moved forward. Soon, it cruised over the white sand beaches and green fields and forests of Hawaii.

"Aloha, Mr. and Mrs. Carr. I'm Alfred Kumura, your pilot for the evening." His voice transmitted loud and clear through the earphones that helped to drown out the engine. He pushed the stick to the side and the craft veered right.

Kumura flew south along the coast, parallel to a long line of sheer cliffs rich with lush vegetation and coffee fields. He pointed the aircraft downward and dove beneath the top of the slopes to catch the sensation of descent from the cliffs onto the beaches at the ocean's edge.

Then he changed course toward the east. The sun tumbled out of sight to the west like a giant red ball about to fall off the edge of the Pacific. Creeping into the dark of night, they ascended to fly over the eastern rift zone of Kilauea.

Progressing slowly, red streams of lava crawled toward the ocean. Fountains of fire shot skyward then fell back toward earth in nature's own fireworks. Nothing he had ever seen compared to the display.

Explosions of flames, dust, and sparks lit the dark sky. Samantha hugged him. "It's so beautiful, Anthony."

At an altitude of about two hundred feet, the pilot navigated parallel to another river of lava as it migrated to the great void of the sea. Molten masses poured out of a lava tube, leaped over a cliff, and fell to the water with a blast of energy, forcing steam high into the air.

The craft pivoted westward. Off in the distance, a series of red lights blinked and darted to and fro in an odd circular pattern.

In seconds, a swarm of other helicopters surrounded the Jet Ranger. Kumura ascended so that he cruised just above the peak of a large cinder cone. He then descended into the three-mile-wide crater. The margin for error was minimal. Beneath them, a boiling red lake of fire and rocks bubbled. The acrid smell of burning sulfur gases permeated the aircraft and made breathing uncomfortable.

Two of the other helicopters followed.

"Don't worry. This cinder cone is an old friend to me. I've done this many times before, you know," the pilot assured them. "We'll be fine."

Anthony gasped for air. Samantha's eyes were frantic, and she clung to him.

Kumura flew lower and lower, until the altimeter read one hundred and fifty-two feet. Intense heat pierced the copter's thin metal skin. Beads of sweat rolled down Anthony's face. This was all wrong. A second craft pulled off, out of sight.

Great curtains of flame and fountains of fire covered the entire depression. The pilot pulled up a hundred feet. The volcano's fierce anger boiled resplendent with hypnotic beauty. From the blinking red lights hovering above, surrounding the volcano's rim, it appeared as if every helicopter in Hawaii had converged at this magnificent scene at this exact moment.

The Gecko Airways chopper began another pass across the lava lake. Fuming red-hot molten rocks cast a glare on the aluminum skins of the helicopters above. Captain Kumura descended to one hundred and thirty-five feet, a risky approach at best.

Samantha shook and held onto Anthony tightly. "Kumura! You're too close! You're scaring us to death." She buried her head in his chest.

"Take it easy, missus. Enjoy this once-in-a-lifetime adventure. Everything will be all right."

Soaked with sweat, Anthony covered her head in his embrace. "Get us out of here. Now! You're too low!"

The craft began to ascend, but before it could gain any altitude, another copter shadowed in the volcanic red hell drew near to them and made a close pass just above their rotor blades.

Agent Allen's warning reverberated in Anthony's mind. It couldn't be.

He leaned forward and poked the pilot. "What is that idiot doing?"

He shook his head. "Not unusual. We get all kinds of traffic out here."

Remaining suspended in space for a brief moment, the other craft stopped, rotated, then flew straight toward them. The Gecko Jet Ranger gained altitude. Anthony's eyes remained glued to the altimeter. They ascended fifty feet straight up and missed the other craft by a few inches.

However, Kumura had very little space to maneuver. He swerved and dipped into a downward vortex. Anthony looked out the window. A rotor blade ever so slightly caught the molten lava. The Jet Ranger cart-wheeled toward the lake like a huge spinning eggbeater.

Samantha screamed.

The aircraft hit the fiery surface. It sat sideways for a brief second, cooking in the bubbling inferno. A fountain of belching rock and fire thrust it into the air and dis-mantled the chopper until little by little it slipped beneath the lava lake and disappeared.

18 The Investigators

Mark Allen threw his fishing box, two freezer chests, and his three favorite rods into the back of his pickup. He kissed a framed picture of his wife and placed it on the passenger seat. Port Aransas on the Texas Coastal Bend had been their secret getaway, and although she died from breast cancer one year ago, he always took her with him.

The most profound regret of his life was that he was on an emergency assignment the night she died. He shook his head. If only he'd returned a day sooner. Being married to the bureau stunk.

A quick stop at his office to check a file, and he was on his way. He slipped in a back entrance to avoid as much contact with the other personnel as he could, but the minute he stooped over his desk, he spotted his secretary. And she obviously spotted him.

She put her hands on her hips. "You should never have come in, but as long as you're here, an agent from Hawaii just called. Something about a helicopter going down a couple of days ago."

Mark winced. "Get him back on the phone right now."

She made the connection, and he picked up. "Mark Allen here. What do you have for me?"

"A tour helicopter went down on the Big Island and the Carrs were aboard. I noticed where you had them under surveillance, what was that about?"

"I'm not at liberty to discuss that right now. What in the world happened?"

"According to eyewitnesses, another helicopter buzzed them and forced a crash into a lava lake."

"Y'all catch the guy?"

"No, he flew off. So far, we haven't even got a clue to go on."

"What about the crash scene? Autopsy done yet?" Mark stared at the ceiling.

"Give me a break. They crashed into the middle of a volcano. There's nothing left of the craft or the bodies."

Mark remained silent several seconds, angry that he didn't exert more pressure on Carr to submit to greater security precautions. Why hadn't the stubborn man listened?

"You still there?" the Hawaiian agent asked.

"Yeah, yeah. If you come up with anything, copy me."

"Glad to."

He hung up the phone, pushed his chair over to his computer bank, punched in his password, then a numerical cipher, and pulled up the beginning of a multi-page folder labeled 'Kappa Gamma Kappa Murders.' Taking a deep breath, he scrolled down several pages, finally reaching a screen with a picture of Anthony Carr.

He typed 'deceased' across the exporter's photograph and shook his head. Pondering how next to proceed, he tapped his pencil on his desk pad. He had to pool every resource available to catch whoever was behind the murders.

Only three fraternity brothers remained alive. He would not lose another one.

He placed a call to his Austin law enforcement buddy. "Hey, John. Thought I'd let you know that Anthony Carr and his wife have been killed in a helicopter crash in Hawaii."

"Hate to hear that."

Mark leaned back and put a hand behind his head. "You free a week from now?"

"Why? What's up?"

"I'd like to get everyone who's worked on these cases together here in Dallas. Match up information."

"Sounds like a plan."

Seven days later, eight law-enforcement officials met in the main conference room at the Dallas FBI office. On the bare white walls, several large placards hung taped in succession.

The name of a murdered member of the Kappa

Gamma Kappa fraternity was written across the top of each, and a photograph appeared below the name of the victim. The location, date of death, occupation, suspected cause, lead investigator, and departments and agencies involved were listed.

Mark called the meeting to order. "I want to thank you for coming and welcome you to Dallas. Each of us has worked on a case involving one or more of these victims. However, we've not all had the opportunity to coordinate information with each other." He walked around the periphery of the room and stopped in front of each photo.

"I want you to introduce yourselves and inform everyone else of your involvement with this investigation. John, here on my right, was the first to start putting this puzzle together."

The short brawny man raised a hand. "I'm Detective Lieutenant John Anderson of the Austin Police Department. I was lead investigator in the Travis Hamilton case."

"Colonel Curtis Oliver, Texas Rangers. I, too, was involved with Hamilton's murder as well as Judge Sherman's." He moved his fingers around the brim of his hat and gave a slight nod.

"Steve Shelton, here. I hail from Fort Worth and was senior investigator for Jackson Freed who was also a personal friend."

The next man wore a wrinkled pair of pants without a tie or jacket. Two thick gold chains dangled from his neck. "Luis Cardona, DEA. Round about, I was involved with Freed's murder investigation trying to nab a Mexican drug lord."

One other FBI agent and two police department detectives completed the circle of investigators.

Mark glanced at each operative. "Now, let's go around again and share what we know. Your theories, too."

Anderson stood. "At the time of the senator's death, we had no reason to link it to other homicides. However, if a connection exists, it may all have begun with events that initially occurred in the Austin area."

Cardona made a grunting noise. "You're talking the fraternity link? Since several of the deceased were also involved in the drug trade, one way or another, I tend to believe that should be our focus."

Anderson unbuttoned his jacket. "Drugs may play a part, but it's the frat connection that interests me."

For the next few minutes each man weighed in on what he thought. Then, each in turn threw out theories. In the end, everyone agreed to keep the others informed.

19 Moving Up The Ladder

Monica and Adam sat at the head table with several other dignitaries in front of a sold-out luncheon audience at the Edinburg Convention Center. She passed her spoon through the last remnants of flan on her dessert plate.

The occasional clattering of silverware and aroma of fresh-brewed coffee floated through the room. At the speaker's podium, the president of the Rio Grande Valley Chapter of the Chamber of Commerce adjusted the microphone.

After he welcomed and introduced all the guests, he finally got to the purpose of the gathering.

"Every year, we give an award to the person whom we feel contributed most to the economy and business climate of our beloved Lower Rio Grande Valley." He smiled. "It is with great pleasure that I present this

Waterford glass trophy to this year's recipient, Congresswoman Monica Gutierrez."

She squeezed Adam's hand tightly. He couldn't have smiled any wider. He kissed her and off she went making her way to the podium. She stopped often grasping hands of the people she served. She climbed the stairs and joined the community leader.

"Thank you." She could hardly believe they had chosen her. "Thank you so much. This is a great honor." She glanced at Adam and winked. She loved him so much. He made her the happiest woman alive.

For the next few minutes, she spoke from her heart without notes.

"To wrap this up, I am so grateful for the opportunity you all have given me to serve my community, my family, my friends and neighbors. I look forward to helping residents of the Valley for years to come as your representative in Congress. Together, we will continue to better the lives of all the people in the Valley."

She waved to the audience, and they responded with a standing ovation. The lights above the podium reflected off the four-carat diamond ring surrounded with sparkling baguettes that Adam had just given her. She held her hands up. "I want to share some wonderful news."

The crowd hushed.

"Adam Cain and I became engaged this morning." She turned her left hand around and pointed to her ring. The crowd applauded.

Late that evening, a phone call from Bentsen Russell surprised Monica. Not the hour, but that she had not spoken to him for almost three months.

"I want you to return to Washington right away. I need to meet with you about a very urgent issue."

She let her head fall back and stared at the ceiling. "That's crazy, Bentsen. I have unfinished business here."

"I need you now. Tonight if possible."

She glanced at Adam. "Mr. Cain is here. Perhaps he can fly me up in the morning, but don't think I'm thrilled about your summons. We were going to Mexico to celebrate our engagement."

Adam's Gulfstream landed at Washington's Reagan International Airport at noon. In a quick twenty minutes, she arrived at Secretary Russell's office where several other Texas congressmen already sat waiting. At least she wasn't the only one. She took the last chair and Adam stood right behind.

"We have a difficult situation in Texas." The secretary rose from his desk and stood in front of her. "Both senators are Republicans. The governor is about to run for president, and the Republican lieutenant governor will take his place. We still have a few congressmen, but the party has lost control of the state."

Bubba Thompson, a stubby little representative from Houston, approached her. "Monica, you're our best chance. We want to run you for lieutenant governor."

She looked around the room at all the aficionados with their determined expressions. "I'm sorry. I don't get it, gentlemen. I'm a second term congresswoman from the Rio Grande Valley. How is it that you expect me to bail out the party?"

"Hear us out." Bubba patted her arm. "You have several winning points. You're a woman, Hispanic, and a supporter of NAFTA. More than half the Texans fit that description. Why, you should be able to carry South Texas, San Antonio, and El Paso easily. And you've got a real good shot at Houston."

He reared back and came down with a hand on Adam's shoulder. "And I'm thinking your new fiancé here can gather more than enough support for the campaign up North."

"Gentlemen. I disagree. When the governor runs for president, he'll bring in every member of his party on his coattails. I won't stand a chance. I can do way more for the people of my district in the house than as a losing candidate."

Russell motioned Bubba to sit down. "You realize that if you refuse, we'll not be obligated to support you for reelection."

She frowned. "Mr. Secretary, I don't appreciate threats. I've enough goodwill in my district to get elected without any of you."

Adam took her by the arm. "Let's get out of here."

She walked out on his arm, leaving the power brokers in stunned silence.

*   *   *   *   *

Early the next morning, he and Monica boarded his Gulfstream for the trip back to McAllen. Charley, a pilot who had been flying with him for only a few months, sat at the controls. Adam fit himself into the copilot seat. Monica climbed into the cockpit's jump seat behind the pilot.

Twenty minutes out of Reagan, the entire craft shuddered and shook.

"Charley! What's going on?" The instruments gyrated erratically.

The pilot checked gauges and flipped switches. "We've got a problem in the right engine."

A loud explosion rocked the right side of the jet. It shook violently and pitched left. Adam hung upside down in his seat. The altimeter turned rapidly as the plane descended. "Eighteen thousand, thirteen thousand, ten thousand. Five thousand. Come on!"

Beads of sweat rolled down Charley's forehead. "Forget the numbers. Work with me. Pull with me. Pull!" He pushed back into his seat and manipulated the controls. His jaws clenched.

"Pull, Charley! As hard as you can, or we're going to lose it. We can do it! Come on, pull!" Every muscle in Adam's body ached. He worked the yoke and pedals. But the ground came faster and faster. Only seconds, and the plane would be in an unrecoverable spin and crash.

Finally, she responded. The shaking and shuddering eased. Charley pulled it into a level flight at three thousand feet.

Adam's eyes cut back to Monica. Her face was ashen. The cockpit smelled of the vomit. It stained her suit. "I hate to ask, but we have our hands full up here, and I need your help. There's a flashlight attached to the cabin just above your head. Remove it."

She nodded and reached for it.

"Good girl. Now I want you to feel the cabin door. If it's hot, don't open it. Otherwise, unlatch it and check out the cabin with your flashlight. You're going to have to undo your seatbelt for a few seconds, and we're still pretty unstable, so be careful."

"The door's cool." She set it ajar, searched the cabin for a few seconds, then closed it. "It's a little hazy, but there's no fire. There's a chunk of metal wedged between the wall and the circular seat in the back." She stumbled back and buckled herself in again. "If anyone was sitting there, it would've killed them."

"Mayday, Mayday." Adam yelled into his mike. "Mayday, Mayday, Washington control. This is Gulfstream N-four-one-zero-five. We've lost an engine. Descending rapidly. Pretty bad vibration. Don't know how long we can hold her together."

"Roger that, Gulfstream. We have you eighteen miles east of Richmond Regional Airport. Do you have enough control to make it there?"

Adam looked at Charley. He nodded. "Affirmative. We've got a visual. Can see it straight ahead."

"Roger that, turning you over to Richmond Tower. Good luck."

"This is Richmond Tower, Gulfstream. You should be eight minutes out. We're clearing the field for you. You're clear for a straight-in landing on runway One-seven east. Our emergency equipment is on the move now. How many souls on board?"

"Three souls."

"Copy that. Good luck and G-d bless."

"Thanks." Adam whispered a prayer.

Monica tapped him softly on the shoulder. "I love you," floated out on the wind of her breath.

The small jet continued to shake and sway. At fifteen feet, Charley cut the good engine. The swaying stopped and the aircraft stayed in line with the runway. The wheels bounced twice, and the jet gradually rolled to a stop surrounded by fire engines and an ambulance.

20 Putting It All Together

On a gray still morning with the tall buildings of down-town Dallas enshrouded in a brown cloud of dust and ozone, Mark Allen waited for the others to arrive.

Soon all were present. Detailing each crime, long sheets of information decorated the bland conference room walls. Photographs of the victims, as well as Adam Cain, Dr. Robert Schwartz, and Rabbi Arnold Weiss, the last surviving fraternity members, rested on individual easels in front of the room.

Mark leaned on a small brown podium and eyeballed each lawman. "Since all the events leading to the Kappa Gamma murders took place in Austin in 1970, Detective Anderson will start."

The lieutenant removed his western cut jacket and walked to the head of the conference table. "Gentlemen, all of these men lived in the same UT frat house. Most became very successful businessmen or professionals. Many had contacts or dealings with people in drug trafficking."

He nodded at Cardona then booted his laptop and turned on a PowerPoint projector. Mark pressed a button, and a white screen descended from the ceiling. The presentation projected images one at a time.

"Let's go to the next document. The *Austin American-Statesman* ran this on May 22, 1970." He ran his red laser beam pointer below each line in the story.

UT Student killed
in hit-and-run accident

A University of Texas student was killed by a hit and run driver during a fraternity prank on an isolated road last night near Mount Bonnell. Austin Police Sergeant Larry Siegert said the victim was Aaron Michaels, eighteen, of Fort Worth. There were few clues and no suspects.

"If anyone saw a red vehicle in the vicinity of Mount Bonnell after midnight, call Austin Police at 512-555-3450," said Siegert.

Anderson clicked through a set of photographs depicting how the murdered men appeared in their youth. Mark moved off to the side to get a better view of the PowerPoint program. "John, what do you know about Aaron Michaels?"

"We never found the person who ran the Michaels kid over. The frat itself didn't take much of a hit either. A one-year suspension. They never really even closed shop. Even kept its charter. The boys involved in the hazing got a year's social probation. No fine. No jail time. No nothing."

Anderson cleared his throat. "They minded their manners for a spell, and most of them graduated, some with honors. Every fraternity member, class of 1970, listed here, played a part in the prank one way or another."

He paused a minute and sipped his coffee, then clicked to the next image. "This kid is Eduardo Menendez from Guadalajara, Mexico. He jumped or was pushed out a second story window.

"Can't say exactly what happened, but the fraternity brothers had blackballed him earlier in the same year. Couldn't keep up with the already low standards of the fraternity." He put a finger to his nose and sniffed.

"The kid took a load of whiskey, LSD, and uppers and went reeling out the window one night. Didn't die, but he become almost a vegetable, a paraplegic. He was hooked to a breathing machine until he died just before his thirty-fifth birthday from complications related to pneumonia."

Cardona snapped his fingers. "Was the Menendez kid related in any way to Pablo Menendez?"

Oliver flicked his Stetson. "Don't rightly know, but I'll bet my boots you could find out right quick."

Cardona pushed away from the conference table, put

an arm around Mark's shoulder and quietly moved him away from the others. "I need a secured non-traceable phone line."

Mark pressed an intercom button on the wall and a middle-aged woman entered. "Take this gentleman to six-three-seven. Here's the key."

She nodded and led Cardona out.

Mark faced Anderson. "What do you have on Aaron Michaels?"

"He listed Thelma Cain of Fort Worth as his mother. Didn't mention a father anywhere. Adam Cain listed Thelma Cain as his mother as well. He, too, failed to list a father."

"So they were related?"

"Aaron turned out to be the son of Thelma Cain's sister. A Braniff Airlines' Electra crashed near Houston and killed his parents when he was four years old—no brothers or sisters. Thelma, as a single mother, raised Adam and Aaron as brothers.

"She died in 1984 after a long bout with breast cancer. A couple of her friends told us she mourned Aaron's death until the end. She never understood why the police couldn't find his killer, or why they never punished the boys who participated in the hazing."

Cardona slipped in with a broad smile. "Bingo! The late Eduardo Menendez was the nephew of the infamous Pablo Menendez of Guadalajara. A wild kid with a lot of money to throw around. A real playboy. Big drinker, drugs, and many, many muchachas.

"Menendez hoped that as Eduardo got older, he'd settle down, lead a more normal life. The entire family regarded the boy as an embarrassment." He sat down.

"Pablo hoped that if he sent Eduardo to a school out of the country, he'd straighten out. None of them thought the kid had any chance of making it, but at least they could get rid of him for a few years, and that in itself would be a blessing."

Cardona poured some water from a decanter and took a sip. "When the boy stepped out of the window at the Kappa Gamma house, his uncle took it very hard and personal, but my man claims the cartel is not involved. Matter of fact, says they blamed the kid more than the frat boys."

Mark ran his fingers through his hair and leaned back in his chair. "Do you really believe that?"

"No, not for a moment. Revenge is a powerful motivation. And—" Cardona shrugged. "The cartel was in Hawaii when the last guy went down."

"Who was it?"

"José Perez. He got to Hawaii a week before the Carrs. Met with a French national, name of Alain Corseau, a.k.a. The Arranger." Cardona shook his head. "Didn't make the connection at the time."

Oliver flicked the brim of his Stetson. "Both of them right on Carr's trail."

Cardona gestured with his hands. "When the cartel pursues a hit, particularly outside of Mexico, Corseau acts as an intermediary and just like that, another one hits the dust. Hardly ever does his own dirty work, though."

Anderson pushed back from the table. "Were any of the surviving fraternity members in Hawaii at the same time as the Carrs?"

Mark nodded. "Schwartz. Vacationing with his family."

"Think there's anything to that?"

"No, we had someone on him the whole time."

"What about the rabbi?"

"Home with his congregation in Fort Worth."

Cardona fidgeted with the largest of his gold chains. "And the last one left standing is Cain. Where was he?"

"With Congresswoman Gutierrez."

Anderson tapped the table. "Cain was there when Hamilton was killed. Was he in Hawaii or in proximity to any of the other murders?"

Mark pointed his laser beam at Cain's photo. "Not that we could find. We looked at his flight logs and questioned his ground crew and checked all commercial flights to Hawaii. If he was, he didn't leave a trail." He took over the PowerPoint presentation. A beautiful old red brick building with a Star of David projected onto the screen, followed by an invitation to a religious event.

"All three survivors will be at the same place at the same time four weeks from this Friday night. Robert Schwartz's son, Tanner, will have his Bar Mitzvah at Temple Israel, near downtown Fort Worth. Rabbi Arnold Weiss will officiate, and Adam Cain has already sent an RSVP.

"My gut tells me we'll not have another reason to get together until the Bar Mitzvah. Plan to be there. We'll be in touch regarding time and place."

As he predicated, no one died nor anything of interest turned up. Two days before the big event, he contacted the others.

"Enter the back door marked vendor delivery at the Federated Laundry and Uniform Rental building on 311 West Reed," he told each in turn. "Come armed, but keep your weapons hidden."

21 There Shall Come A Blood Avenger

At seventeen hundred hours, on a breezy Friday evening, a red Ford Crown Victoria parked two blocks north of the old dilapidated laundry building.

Mark Allen and two of his agents walked through the old neighborhood of ancient run-down warehouses and factories, their doors and windows accented by heavy steel bars. The air wafted with the smell of cottonseed oil from an extractor a few blocks away.

He reached the weatherbeaten building four blocks from Temple Israel. Three large, round, metallic ventilation pipes extruded through the laundry's outside walls and rose three stories across the worn gray facade, joining in a triangle at the apex of the roof.

The rusted oval conduits periodically expelled short puffs of white smoke. Above an eight-foot chain-link fence topped with razor wire, a sign read: "Federated

Uniform Rental and Laundry."

Arriving at their allocated times, the others entered through the front gate and meandered to the rear door. An enormous wooden meeting table with twelve chairs occupied the center of the room where a PowerPoint projector sat on a moveable rack. Detergent, starch, and nitrate odors permeated even this isolated section of the old building.

Illuminating two large architectural schematic plans, a large center light with a green shade dangled from the ceiling. Mark stood in front of one set of drawings depicting the inside of Temple Israel in minute detail. He pointed out each entrance, exit, light switch, fuse box, roof, and staircase.

The other, a map off to his side, detailed surrounding streets as well as ingress and egress to major highways, interstates, and ancillary arteries.

He welcomed the members of his team, and their individual conversations ceased. "Our objective is to foil any assassination attempt before it occurs. This'll require astute observation and exacting execution on the part of every person in this room.

"More than three hundred people should attend the Schwartz Bar Mitzvah. The last thing we need is any unnecessary loss of life." He picked up a small device and displayed it. "A radio receiver. Please open the small black box in front of each of you. As you can see, no outside wires, and it's about the size of a small pea."

Mark pushed it into his ear with his pinkie, and the

other law enforcement officers in the room followed suit with the exception of Cardona.

He looked down at the tiny skin-colored instrument. "Small suckers, aren't they? Looks like they might get lost in your ear real easy like. How do you get them out?"

"With a surgical tweezers and a suction device. Don't worry, we use these beauties all the time. Won't hurt a bit." A female agent in the back of the room answered, "Aren't afraid, are you?"

Mark waved his hands. "All right, listen up, and cut the chatter. We've got a lot of ground to cover. The watches on the table have a small transmitting unit."

Fastening the black-banded device onto his wrist, he raised it in the air. "Don't use it unless a life or death situation presents itself. I'll give all commands and position myself in a way so I can see everyone clearly. Each of you will reply with a whisper only on my command. Otherwise, acknowledge reception with one affirmative nod."

Anderson looked up. "What if it doesn't work? Do we have an alternative system?"

"We've arranged for a backup to sit next to each of you, but the bureau's used this system many times. Complete failure has never occurred."

He put his finger into his ear to make sure the device was secure. "Time to check the equipment. An agent on another floor in this building will call each of you by your last name. If the receiver works properly, respond by saying 'reception positive' into the speaker."

Each operative confirmed that the equipment was fully operational.

Placing the document containing the architectural schemata of the temple onto an oversized street map, Mark used a laser pointer and zeroed in on various details. "Temple Israel's bounded by West Main and Claremont, four blocks east of our present location.

"We have the good fortune of having a total of only three exit and entry points. One in front of the building and the other two within one hundred feet of each other on the left side toward the middle of the structure.

"On most Sabbath evenings, the congregation employs two security guards. Both on duty tonight are agents dressed in Leary Security Service uniforms. In addition, we'll station two cars with agents across the street from the temple, one positioned on the side street and the other on the avenue that runs parallel to the building."

Anderson twisted in his seat and alternately tapped his fingers on the table several times. "Two cars enough if someone does a hit and makes a run?"

"It should do, but we've got backup with an additional vehicle posted one block away. Also the DEA has supplied us with a helicopter equipped with high-tech electronic devices and night vision. No one will get away."

Taking a deep breath, the Austin detective exhaled slowly. "You're in command, but I still don't know about the external surveillance plan."

He ignored Anderson's remarks. "We'll enter in pairs through different doors. Two of my agents will follow me in the front and sit in the last row of the balcony. It's recessed and doesn't cantilever out over the first floor seating area. I'll sit in the front row. That should provide a good view of the entire ground floor of the sanctuary."

Mark paused and pointed with a laser beam to the architectural rendering that detailed the seating pattern. "John and Curtis will come in on this first side door and sit here on the aisle three rows behind and to the right of the front stage, or bema, as it's called in a temple." He pointed his finger at the Texas Ranger. "And by the way, Curtis, get rid of your Stetson. It's a great looking hat, but you'd stand out like a sore thumb.

"Shelton and Cardona, I want you to use the same entrance and sit here in the exact same location as John and Curtis except on the left side."

Mark pointed to his last two FBI agents. "Sit in the middle of the last row of the downstairs section. Everyone clear on positioning?"

They all nodded.

"Now some other important characteristics of the building." He pointed to various features on the schematic drawings. "First of all, the temple has a basement. After the ceremony, the family will host a reception in that area. It's got two entry points: a stairwell near the first side door and another just to the left of the bema.

"Two of our agents are serving, a waiter and busboy.

They'll be stationed in the basement from the get-go, arranging chairs, tables, food trays, and the like."

His pointer glided along the plans. When the ceremony's finished, Doctor Schwartz, his family, and the rabbi will form a line just in front of the staircase to greet the guests before they make their way downstairs for the party. The left front door to the side of the bema in the sanctuary is usually locked and egress cannot be made from there to the room below."

His eyes cut to the Austinites. "I want Curtis and John between the reception line and side door about ten feet away when the service concludes. Our agents outside will remain in front of the same door."

Next, he sauntered over to Shelton and Cardona. "You two linger in the sanctuary and guard the left side door to the basement. Go on part way down if the door's open for any reason, but stay there to protect that point of entry just in case there are any surprises.

"The two agents assigned to the rear center of the sanctuary will wait for the entire crowd to leave before joining the end of the reception line. He hit two other agents in the chest with his red laser. "You and I will keep to the balcony until all the subjects clear the area and then join the party."

Anderson wore a scowl.

"You got a problem, John?"

"What about the stairs to the balcony?"

"A legitimate question. I'll make sure they're covered by those assisting me."

"Then I think you've touched all the bases."

Mark nodded. "Not quite finished yet. Someone hit the lights and turn on the PowerPoint."

The lights dimmed, and a laptop computer flashed an image of Adam Cain in an arm cast on the blank wall in front of the room.

"Pay close attention. Your lives and those of any intended victims will depend on your ability to make rapid identification of each of these people and take appropriate action.

"Cain had a horseback-riding accident a couple of weeks ago, broke his right arm and has a cast. Congresswoman Monica Gutierrez, his fiancée, will accompany him to the Bar Mitzvah."

Monica's picture projected on the wall with more information. Photographs of Dr. Schwartz and his family, Rabbi Weiss, his wife, and their two daughters followed.

"This last group shows known members of the assassination team. The first is Alain Corseau, who arranges the financing and recruits gunmen for the Guadalajara cartel's hits." Mark pointed out the man's distinctive snow-white forelock in front of his blond hair then moved on to the next picture.

"José Perez, a senior cartel captain, is short, about five-six. He and Corseau are usually in close proximity. And here's Gregg Foster. He's a hired hand for the Mexican Mafia." Mark directed his laser across a four-inch scar just above the man's left eye.

"Last but not least, is Little Joe Hernandez. A local boy from Haltom City. He's murdered all over the world. Usually wears a dark shirt with a light-colored suit and tie." When Mark finished the presentation, he gazed around the room. "Questions?"

No one spoke up.

"Everyone set then?"

The lawmen nodded and a few shouted, "Yes, sir."

"Then let's saddle up, and get on with it."

22 The Bar Mitzvah

Who are my people?

I don't know if I should share my innermost feelings with you.

I used to try and stop them, but I can't anymore. Man, do they give me a headache. Makes my brain feel like it's tied in a knot. Like a whole bunch of radio and TV stations, all playing at the same time.

They used to make me feel real bad. No more, because I need to take good care of them, and they'll take good care of me.

You really want to know. Don't you? Okay, let's share my deepest darkest secrets. But, shhh. You can't tell anyone. I think I can trust you.

They're present almost all the time now. My inner and outer voices, that's who. They tell me what to do, who the victims should be, and how carry it out. These clever voices always work out a way. Sometimes I can control them and sometimes not. Never know when.

But I always check things out with my mother in heaven, blessed be she. Sometimes she consults with the devil before she answers me. Oh, you don't believe in the devil? He's always there, always. She calls all the shots once she talks to him.

Soon, she'll be satisfied and rest in peace. As for me, I'll either be here on earth finally free of my obligations or dead. Don't know which I like better. Dead free, free dead, dead free, dead me. Anyway, it will be over soon and my torture will end.

*   *   *   *   *

Mark entered the front doors of Temple Israel, an oasis of beauty and charm in a neighborhood of dereliction and decay. An usher welcomed him, gave him a prayer book, and wished him a good Sabbath. The temple was filled to capacity. The remainder of the team filtered into the main sanctuary with the other guests.

Soft lights bathed the beautiful stained glass windows, casting a warm glow that conveyed a sense of faith, history, and time. Accentuating the pale gray walls and semicircular rows of coral cushioned seats, small ceramic stars of David with tiny light bulbs floated at varying levels from the ceiling and illuminated the congregation with gentle rays of light.

The bema, a raised stage-like area constructed of

natural hardwoods that shone from a high-lacquered finish, was at the front of the temple. On top of it sat a wide based lectern. Embellishing the back of it, a large structure of glistening marble formed an arc. Above the arc of the Torahs hung two large granite tablets inscribed with the Ten Commandments chiseled in Hebrew.

At seven fifty-five in the evening, just before the start of the Sabbath service, the organ in the balcony played a slow, soulful melody. It set a peaceful mood that belied the undercurrent of what might become a deadly situation.

Only the beating rotors of the DEA's helicopter passing at ten-minute intervals interrupted Mark's tranquil mood. But although he was aware, he figured most the celebrants didn't notice the noise at all. Sitting front and center in the balcony, he surveyed the ground floor then the rows behind him.

With the exception of one blind spot, his balcony view would suffice. His two best men covered the area behind him from the last row center. He studied the congregation and the late-arriving guests as they entered.

Cain and the congresswoman sat near the aisle, four rows behind Oliver and Anderson. Mark whispered into his speaker and informed the two Austin lawmen of the couple's location. Anderson nodded.

Mark spotted Corseau wearing a white and blue knitted skullcap. José Perez, Menendez's senior vice-president, accompanied him. Mark didn't recognize any other members of the Mexican Mafia. Just to play safe, he

communicated with the agent behind him. She confirmed that no one suspicious was in his blind spot.

How odd. Usually Corseau and Perez didn't show up
together anywhere near an assassination attempt, and
particularly not in the absence of other members of the
cartel's hit team. His heart quickened as he pondered the
situation. Why now in such a public place?

Then came a piece of good luck. Corseau and Perez
sat in the third row left side of the auditorium in front of
Shelton and Cardona, so close that they could almost
reach out and touch.

Mark spoke into his wristwatch. "Don't look now.
Corseau and Perez are seated directly in front of you. If
either of them at any time during the service reaches into
his jacket or rises at an inappropriate time, grab him with
both arms and don't let go."

Both lawmen nodded, acknowledging the instructions.

The organist played a more upbeat tune, and the choir
sang in response. The lights dimmed. Rabbi Arnold
Weiss led a processional. The cantor, Dr. Schwartz and
his family followed from the side door and walked up
the three steps to the bema. Schwartz's daughter and
mother-in-law stood near the Sabbath candles.

The rabbi and cantor moved to the podium. Weiss
raised a hand. "Welcome to Temple Israel for our
Sabbath services and the bar mitzvah of Tanner
Schwartz. We are happy to have all of you here with us
this evening. I would now like to call forward Tanner's

mother, Barbara, to join with her daughter, Ashley, and Tanner's grandmother, Mrs. Yetta Goldman, to bless the Sabbath candles."

The women stood at a small side table where two large bronze candleholders contained tall, unlit white candles. Yetta stood in the middle flanked by her daughter and granddaughter. Mrs. Schwartz lit both candles.

The elderly grandmother bent over the circle of light cast by them, her small frame only inches from the flame. She touched her forehead and then spread her arms, fingers barely touching one another in as wide a circle as she could make. She repeated this twice more, then the three women repeated in unison, "Blessed art Thou, oh Lord our G-d, King of the universe who commands the lighting of the Sabbath candles."

The organ played an introduction in a minor key, and the choir followed singing melodically in Hebrew. The congregation's mood seemed peaceful and joyous except for Mark and his team members.

After the initial blessings, the rabbi neared the portion of the liturgy where he would give Tanner Schwartz the honor of leading the congregation in prayer. "It would be wonderful if we had an attendance this large every Friday night. However, I know most of you are here to honor Tanner and the Schwartz family for the bar mitzvah. Many here are from different religious backgrounds.

"Therefore, before I turn things over to Tanner, I would like our visitors to understand how bar mitzvahs came to pass." The rabbi smiled at his audience. "In the ancient days of the Bible, there was not really a rabbi who conducted services as we know them today.

"Oh, there was a leader, all right. However, during the recitation of prayers, each member of a congregation would read a portion of the liturgy then pass the text to the next person so that each adult would read a portion of the service.

"When a young man was considered old enough to take the responsibility of reading prayers with the other congregants, he also participated in the ceremonial daily prayers and was given a portion to read. In most cases, this occurred around the twelfth or thirteenth birthday."

The rabbi raised his hands toward the audience. "When Jews were forced to leave the land of Israel, and they migrated out into the Diaspora—those lands outside of Israel—this event became a marker of the time when a young boy was expected to take his place in the community. He would take on all the attendant responsibility that the occasion implied.

"The bar mitzvah became more and more elaborate with time. In modern days, this very happy event is most often associated with a formal service, a large celebratory dinner and lavish party."

The rabbi turned toward the boy and nodded. "Now with this in mind, I am honored to turn the reading of the Sabbath service over to Tanner."

Young Schwartz had some difficulty peering over the lectern. Stepping onto a small stool scooted into place, he stood next to the cantor and began to read both in English and Hebrew. He smiled and happily accompanied the cantor and choir when they sang their portions. His high-pitched tenor, nearer the microphone, rang out above the rest.

Mark smiled. The young man's voice hadn't changed yet. He continued to scan the temple. A few minutes after Tanner started his portion of the ceremony, Corseau rose from his seat and faced the podium. He stared in Dr. Schwartz's direction, but his hands remained at his side. He made no attempt to reach inside his jacket, although the bulge of a shoulder holster was evident.

"Grab him, grab him now before he does any damage," Mark whispered into his wristwatch.

Some folks around him glanced over. The woman next to him put a finger over her lips. "Shhh."

He smiled at the old lady. "Sorry, I'm a physician on call. Isn't technology wonderful? I can communicate with the hospital any time I need to."

Mark expected the worst and couldn't understand why Cardona didn't seize the man. The agent rose as Corseau made his way to the aisle and followed him step by step. The Frenchman turned to his left as he reached the bema and cast another sinister glance at Schwartz.

*   *   *   *   *

Cardona shadowed him past the bema. As Corseau exited the sanctuary's right door, he continued pursuit into the hallway. Halfway down the corridor, the Frenchman entered the men's room then a stall. Cardona made the pretense of using the urinal, waited a few minutes then flushed, but the Arranger remained behind the closed door.

As he backed out of the men's room, Cardona spotted a classroom across the hall with a small window framed in a wooden door. He slipped inside and waited for his man to leave. His subject might be picking up or assembling a more powerful weapon.

He lifted his wrist. "Hey, Mark. Bet you're pretty pissed off, but every now and then, you gotta freelance. Grabbing the guy would've blown our cover plus created a disturbance. He's in the john, and I'm still on him."

The director didn't reply. Cardona smiled, didn't expect an answer anyway. Soon enough, the men's room door opened. His pulse quickened as he slipped out unnoticed to stay with his prey. He almost hoped the killer felt the breath of his presence.

If not, Perez should notice and would tell him as soon as he sat back down. A chance Cardona had to take. Corseau could have stopped at the bema and shot the rabbi and Dr. Schwartz both at close range, but he didn't. Maybe he just had to go after all.

The Frenchman's pace quickened as he neared his seat. He turned his head and nodded.

Pushing a foot through an opening in the bottom of the chair in front of him, Cardona swift kicked the Arranger to let him know he was being watched.

*   *   *   *   *

Outside the temple, an FBI agent tugged at the ill-fitting and itchy collar of his Leary Security Service shirt. He patrolled back and forth between the parking lot and the temple. From the north, a figure emerged from the darkness.

A dim street lamp illuminated an elderly person pushing a cart containing a bulky package.

The agent spoke into the microphone on his wrist. "Agent Charles, please acknowledge."

"Yeah, Jones? I'm in the middle of a taco, here. What's up?"

"A subject pushing a cart is headed my direction from two blocks north. How about you circle and come up behind him?"

"Will do."

The subject seemed oblivious and continued on a path that would intersect Jones' position. As he got closer, Jones could tell the guy was only a poorly dressed, foul-smelling senior citizen in a shaggy raincoat. The man came to an abrupt stop and tried to move around him, but each time, Jones fronted him again.

"What're you doing here, old man?" He grabbed the cart with one hand and held it in place.

The stranger tried to pull loose. "What makes you think it's any of your business. And just who do you think you are stopping me this way?"

"Agent Hassan Jones of the Federal Bureau of

Investigation."

The toothless old street person laughed until he doubled over. "Yeah, yeah, yeah. And I'm George Washington."

Jones let go of the wagon, reached into his jacket with one hand and toward his holster with his other then whipped out his badge and pistol in one quick motion. He pointed his revolver at the ragged man. "Hold it right there, and keep your hands on top your head in clear sight."

"Why, lookee there, he's got himself a big gun. You ain't got no right to do this." He placed his hands on top of his head. "That's what it's come to. Shooting old men for living on the streets."

The smelly senior citizen's stinking attitude didn't phase Jones in the least. "Now with your left hand, slowly open your plastic bag. No quick movements. Understand? 'Cause I'll have to shoot you."

"I ain't moved quick in more than forty years, but I've done nothing wrong! You can't do this! I got my rights." He fumbled one-handed with the bag's edges.

"Just do what you're told, and no one gets hurt."

"Humph! Think I care? Go ahead and shoot me." The street person threw both hands in the air and glared.

Out of the corner of his eye, Jones saw Agent Charles slip behind the suspect and put the cold steel of her Glock revolver in the middle of his back. "Do exactly as my partner says."

"Oh, so there's two of you. Well, open it yourself if

you want to see what's inside!"

"Open it. Now!" Jones shoved the wagon into the guy.

"Psshaw. Open it or shoot me, I don't care which. I ain't taking no orders from you. FBI, my foot!"

The gray-haired thug crossed his arms over his chest. Jones glanced at Charles then pulled back the plastic. A canvas bag was underneath. He unzipped it slowly. The streetlight's dim illumination glistened off metal.

He unbuckled a flashlight hanging on his waistband and shined it inside the bag. The old man was packing a machine pistol, an Uzi, and the broken-down stock, barrel, and muzzle of a sawed-off shotgun.

Charles raised her eyebrows. "Good grief! What are you doing with all that firepower?"

"Told you! I live in the street. Need to protect m'self, don't I?" The old man's face drew taut and his smirk disappeared.

Shaking his head, Jones chuckled. "Not with that much firepower, fella. You just earned yourself a warm cot at the county jail tonight."

Charles holstered her Glock. "Look, we're here as a part of a federal stakeout. Cooperate, or you'll wind up doing a lot more time than just for state charges."

"I ain't saying nothin' till I see a lawyer."

Jones read him his Miranda and then cuffed him. At the waiting bureau cruiser, he ran the old man's I.D. and found an extensive record including petty larceny, illegal weapons sales, and forgery. No violent crimes or any connections with the cartel showed up.

＊　　＊　　＊　　＊　　＊

Inside the temple, Mark put down his prayer book and eyed the audience. The service seemed to be coming to a climax.

Rabbi Weiss approached the podium and joined Tanner and the cantor. He raised his hands. "We come to the most important part of our service for the honoree. I will ask the congregation to stand as we open the arc to take out our holy torah."

The congregation stood as the doors in front of the arc opened. Behind them were six scrolls wrapped in what looked to be a fine silk fabric of blue, white and maroon topped with silver crowns. The rabbi removed the largest of the six torahs.

He helped balance it in the grandmother's hands who placed it in the hands of her son Dr. Schwartz who handed the holy scroll to his wife Barbara who in turn gave it to her son.

"And so it is, throughout the ages, from generation to generation, that we have passed down the word and law."

Removing the silver crowns and silk cover, the rabbi laid the torah over the podium. "The torah records the early history of the Jewish people and includes the laws and traditions relative to how Jews should live and conduct themselves toward their fellow man. It contains all of the five books of Moses."

He untied a cloth binder with obvious care and sepa-

rated the rolled wooden ends so that the text lay open
then lifted the scrolls so that the written pages faced the
congregation.

"A very pious rabbi or scribe who follows the law to
the ultimate degree writes every page by hand with a
quill pen on parchment in this sacred document. It usually takes almost a year to complete. As some of you in
the front row can see, there are no vowels, and Tanner
must read his portion without the benefit of these gram-
matical markers."

He signaled to the boy and he began his recitation
with a charming melodic refrain. He performed very
well as far as Mark could tell. Sounded great to him.

When the teen finished his reading, Rabbi Weiss patted his back. "Well done! Not a single mispronunciation.
That was wonderful, Tanner. You were perfect. All your
hard work has really paid off.

"Now I am going to interpret for our guests, from
Hebrew into the English."

The rabbi took a silver pointer shaped like a hand
with a pointed finger and touched each word as he trans-
lated for the congregation:

"You shall set aside cities in
the land that God gives you
to possess so that any

manslayer will have a place relatively nearby that he may run to. Now this will be a place where a manslayer who escapes may be able to live in peace. This is one who had killed another unwittingly without being his enemy in the past.

For example, a man goes with a friend out into the orchard to cut trees. As he begins to chop, the head of his ax separates from the handle and hits the other man, inflicting a wound that kills his friend.

That man may flee to one of these three safe cities, so that he may live. Otherwise, *when the distance is too long, the BLOOD AVENGER pursuing the manslayer may in the heat of anger overtake and kill this person who is not actually guilty of murder. He should not have received the death penalty as he had never been the other man's enemy and killed him only by accident. That is why I, The Lord, command you to set aside these cities. In this manner the blood of the innocent will not be let, and bring a blood guilt upon your land.*

On the other hand, when a man's enemy lies in wait for him and attacks him, delivering a fatal blow, this is different. When he attempts to go to one of these safe cities, the elders of the dead man's community will have the right to bring the murderer back from the safe city and shall hand him over to the nearest surviving relative, THE BLOOD AVENGER, *to be put to death."*

When the rabbi finished translating the passage, the temple president re-dressed the torah in its silk gown and covered the top with the silver crowns. Weiss returned it to the ark and placed it next to the other scrolls.

Facing the ark the rabbi raised his hands high into the air. "The Lord your G-d said, 'Behold, I have given you a good doctrine. Follow its ways and it shall forever be to you as a tree of life.'" And then he closed the doors of the ark.

Weiss stood at the podium and looked out at his congregation. "In a sense, this early reference to capital

punishment provides a judicial system to decide the
guilt or innocence of a given slayer. However, if modern
man followed this dictum fanatically, we would soon
decay into a vigilante society.

"Indeed, later the passage dictates that one should not
bear false witness, and that more than one person needs
to witness a crime before a rabbinical court can declare a
person guilty.

"Unfortunately, it concludes with the more well-
known statement, 'an eye for an eye, a hand for a hand,
a tooth for a tooth, and a life for a life.' As a famous play-
wright once noted, 'If we followed this dictum to the
letter, we would wind up with a good part of the world
that is unpopulated, toothless, and blind.'"

Snickers and giggles waved over the sanctuary.

The rabbi sat down, and the choir sang a soft inter-
lude. When they finished, Weiss moved to the podium
again and motioned Tanner to join him.

There, he faced the boy. "Your voice was wonderful,
your reading exacting, and the congregation takes great
pride in how you conducted the services and Torah reading." He turned then to the people. "It took Tanner many
years of hard work and study to achieve this wonderful
moment. Now he has a few words of his own for his
family about this meaningful evening."

The young boy followed with a brief speech about the
significance of his bar mitzvah and thanked the members of his family, the rabbi, and his teachers for their
help and support.

The president of the temple brotherhood awarded Tanner a silver cup to use as part of the Sabbath prayer ceremonies at home. He then made several announcements and invited everyone to an Oneg Shabbat, a post-Sabbath reception given by Dr. and Mrs. Robert Schwartz in the basement parlor immediately after the final prayers.

When the temple president sat down, the rabbi raised his arms. "May the Lord bless you and keep you. May He cause His countenance to shine upon you. And may He grant you shalom, peace, the greatest gift of all."

Anderson turned to Oliver and raised both hands, wrists near his mouth as though stretching. "Well, looks like it's almost over, and we're home free." Mark winced. That wasn't like John. Jumping to such conclusions could only bring disaster.

Oliver shook his head. "Ain't over till it's over."

After the service, the congregation waited a few minutes until the rabbi, cantor, and Schwartz family left the sanctuary and formed a receiving line in the hall just in front of a small staircase leading to the downstairs parlor. Then the congregants began their exodus into the hallway.

As previously designed in the operational plan, Anderson and Oliver positioned themselves between the receiving line and the side door. Adam and Monica pushed through the exit just a little bit later.

Mark noted that rather than joining the worshippers who waited to congratulate the family, Corseau and Perez stayed in the far left aisle of the temple and conversed.

Cardona and Shelton placed themselves at the left door from the sanctuary leading to the basement. The two agents at the rear of the balcony joined the end of the receiving line, and only then did Mark leave his command position and saunter down the staircase to the sanctuary floor.

*   *   *   *   *

The first folks in line greeted the host family and clergy then moved on. Cain followed closely behind, separated from Monica by two couples who had moved between them. He shook hands with Yetta Goldman and spoke to her briefly then smiled and stepped on toward the cantor.

Anderson maneuvered enough to overhear Cain. While he listened, he studied the man's broken arm and tried to picture him on a horse. The cast looked unusually angulated. Only a small portion of his thumb remained uncovered.

It didn't look like any arm cast he'd ever seen. His heartbeat pounded like a stalking lion waiting to pounce.

Cain leaned in and hugged Barbara Schwartz with his good arm. "I know how proud you are of Tanner. He sure seems like a fine son." He stood erect, but held onto her hand, shaking it methodically. "Haven't seen you and Robert in quite a while. We need to get together soon."

Barbara nodded. "Sounds like a good idea. I'll call
Monica and set a date."

He shook Robert's left hand. "Left handshakes are
always the best, because they are closer to the heart."

Staring at Rabbi Weiss with his cold steel gray eyes,
Cain placed his lower lip between his teeth and pulled it
back against them. Anderson had seen that movement
before, but where? When? The rabbi took Cain's good
hand and shook it firmly. They appeared happy to see
one another.

"Things seem to be going well for you and the congregation," he said.

The rabbi nodded. "Very well, indeed. I want to tell
you how much we appreciate your financial support, but
would really like to see more—"

Anderson lunged forward, bolted through the line
and tackled Cain waist high. He and his target somer-
saulted down the staircase. The force of the tackle and
combined weights propelled him and Cain down the
metal stairs, banging him into walls. He rolled onto the
basement floor first.

His head struck a small table with a thud. A tremen-
dous pain thundered through his brain. Cain's cast broke
open from the force of the fall, but somehow he was able
to hold onto the revolver in his right hand. He came to
rest on the ground, his gun aimed at Anderson who
stood above him just inches away.

Cain released the safety and fired, but Anderson

rolled right, and in one simultaneous motion pulled his Beretta from his back holster. The heat of a bullet grazed Anderson's cheek, and the smell of gunpowder singed his nostrils.

On the floor, he lost sight of Cain for a split second. Then he fired two shots. One found its mark and hit Cain in the chest. He groaned and rolled onto his side. The revolver fell out of his open hand. Anderson looked up the stairs.

Schwartz pushed his family to the ground and threw his body full-length across them. The people already in the hall panicked. Some froze in place. Others dropped to the floor. A few screamed. In a state of confusion, several ran around in all different directions.

Monica raced down the stairs before anyone could stop her. She ran to her beloved and knelt beside him. "Adam! Adam! Are you all right?"

Oliver followed close behind, revolver drawn. Allen arrived a few seconds later, and ordered two agents to the side door. "Cordon off that area! Between the hall and stairs!"

Blood spewed from a gaping hole in Cain's chest. The dying man lay on his back on the carpeted parlor floor now stained with blood. Anderson stood over him, his Beretta in both hands at the ready.

Monica looked up at him. "Have you gone mad? What have you done, you idiot!" She held Cain's face in her hands and wept over him. "Adam, don't leave me! Do you hear? Don't you dare leave me!"

He gasped for air. "Monica, I love you."

"I love you, too, my darling." She gave him a soft kiss. "I love you, too. Hang on." She scanned the room full of now gawking spectators. "Don't just stand there. Someone call an ambulance!"

"Monica? Monica, I've got to tell you something." His muffled words were soft. She leaned closer to hear. Blood bubbled up and over his lips. "She made me. They killed Aaron, and no one—no one paid." He struggled for a breath and winced.

"Who, darling? Who made you?"

His voice weakened, he paused between words. "My—my—my mother. She made me. No one paid. She made me promise."

Monica shook her head as though unable to understand the brevity of his truths. "Promise what, Adam?"

"To kill them. They had to pay. Someone had to avenge Aaron. It was wrong, but I—I—I promised her." He grabbed Monica's neck and pulled her closer. "She was d—dy—ing." His voice grew fainter with each syllable. Then fell silent.

Monica screamed at Anderson between sobs. "You killed him! You idiot! You killed him!"

Anderson took a deep breath, bowed his head, but did not reply. He did his duty and didn't owe an explanation to anyone except to the director of the operation.

She stared at Cain lying motionless on the floor. Her mouth contorted, mascara-streaked tears ran down, staining her face. "What just happened? I don't understand."

Allen put his arm around her shoulders and offered comfort. "If Detective Anderson hadn't stopped him, he would've killed Rabbi Weiss."

"But why? Who had to pay? And for what?"

Anderson nodded and swallowed hard. "We think there were several others, including your old boss, Senator Hamilton."

"Travis?" She accepted Allen's hand and stood, leaning hard against him, still visibly shaken. "But why? How could he?" She sobbed.

"All part of a very twisted story. He just wasn't in his right mind."

She looked down at him. "I'm sorry, I've got to get out of here."

Allen took her by the arm and escorted her to the door leading from the basement to the street. "We'll want to talk to you later." Monica nodded as she walked out into the cool evening air. Rabbi Weiss hurried out after her.

The director looked at Anderson and offered a slight smile. "How did you know?"

He shook his head and raised his hands, palms up. "I didn't, exactly. A guy name of Leon Czolgos assassinated President McKinley with a gun hidden in a cast. The shape of Cain's cast didn't look right, and he carried it strange. Not really like anyone I'd seen with a broken arm.

"Cain also did something funny with his mouth. I'd seen it before, just after our interview when he murdered

Hamilton. Guess I followed my gut." He shrugged. "And guessed right."

"What if you were wrong?"

He turned around. "In that case, Steve, he'd have sued me and you would've had to find me one real fine lawyer."

*   *   *   *   *

In the sanctuary, Cardona had kicked in the side door when the commotion started and ran down to the basement. Perez and Corseau followed, but turned back halfway and beat a hasty retreat toward the front. Cardona followed and caught a hold of Corseau's jacket just as he opened the door.

"Hey, hey. What's the hurry, gentlemen?"

Perez stopped, turned and offered a faint grin. The door slowly closed itself. "Ah, you see, we are done here."

"Done? Done with what?"

"Your people got Cain and took care of our business. Gracias, amigo. Thank you for saving us the trouble."

Cardona followed the two men through the huge outer doors. They headed down the street toward a well-guarded limousine.

He called after them, "Keep looking over your shoulders, gentlemen. I'll be there."

Epilogue

Headed toward Pristina, U.S. Ambassador-at-Large Bentsen Russell sat in the rear seat of a Humvee as it struggled down a steep mountain on a narrow, shell-pocked road. Death and ethnic hatred surrounded him on all sides.

Howitzer and mortar shells intermittently screamed over the vehicle and reverberated the night air with explosive force from the city below. Scattered small weapons and machine-gun fire crackled from every direction.

It delighted Russell that the president chose him as chief negotiator in Kosovo. Negotiating cease-fires at three separate sites wasn't bad for a day's work. However, driving over hostile terrain and conferencing with Serbs and the Kosovo Liberation Army had worn down his patience.

Exhausted, he slouched in the back seat and closed his eyes, intermittently dozing off. At least when he reached

Pristina he could get some good sleep.

He paid little attention to the two soldiers in the front seat. Their conversation was of no interest, and listening kept him awake. He just wanted to rest. He sighed and stared out the window. Crossing the crest of the mountain in the daytime, the entire city would be appearing any minute. But darkness prevailed over the night, and nothing showed other than the shadows of buildings illuminated by the light of exploding shells.

The driver eased the Hummer around a curve heading down the mountain road made slick from an all-day rain. The vehicle picked up speed. Russell's stomach suddenly felt hollow and queasy. Heading into a tighter curve, the Hummer lost traction.

Brakes ground, but like a drunken dancer, the vehicle slipped beyond the edge of the narrow road and flew into the air like a chunk of lead. Russell wet his pants. He pushed against the front seat to brace himself and grabbed for the seat belt. Was this it? Was his life over?

His head hit the roof. He grimaced and shuddered from the blow. Must be upside down. He was being tossed like a rag doll. The passenger up front screamed for his mother.

At the bottom of a ravine, the force of the tumbling vehicle thrust him to the floor. Finally the motion stopped. How amazing that the vehicle hadn't exploded. At least he thought he was still alive.

He must be. His legs hurt worse than he could have ever imagined. It wouldn't hurt if he were dead, right?

Horrendous pain raced through every part of his being. The men in the front climbed out screaming something to one another. Russell tried to lift the hunk of metal that pinned his legs, but no matter how hard he pulled, it wouldn't budge.

"Help me! Help!"

Then he saw it. A rough-edged white bone protruded through his torn skin. His stomach rolled. He vomited.

His body shook, soaked in urine and sweat. His breath became rapid and shallow. Even if it meant crawling out, digging with his bare hands, he had to get rid of whatever pinned him down. He screamed again for help. Where had the soldiers gone?

Leaking gasoline fumes fouled the air. He glanced at the flickering yellow sparks behind him that illuminated the darkness like a thousand fireflies. Then suddenly, a great wall of bright, orange flame engulfed him.

"Help! Get me out of here! I'm burning! I'm burning!"

Suddenly, all the pain ended. He passed through a tunnel of lights, out of the earth's womb.

The president ordered Ambassador Russell's body flown back to the United States by a military aircraft, and he was buried with full honors at Arlington National Cemetery. When attorneys settled his estate, they sold his beloved Texas ranch.

The new owners cleared sections of the vast acreage in preparation for an exotic hunting and fishing resort.

They named one project "Fisherman's Paradise Lake." Its construction included deepening a large stock pond near the back of the property. Twelve feet from shore, the dredge operator struck a large solid object. Divers identified it as a vehicle.

The job foreman hooked a steel cable to the thing, and slowly a submerged automobile rose to the surface.

An old rusted red Pontiac Grand Prix surfaced. The slimy, battered car came to rest on the shore. The right headlamp was broken and a large dent on the right bumper seemed to have remnants of decayed cloth embedded in it.

*   *   *   *   *

Captain Anderson sat at his desk at Austin's homicide division headquarters. He sorted papers trying to close out the day. He stretched his shoulders. Couldn't wait to get home to Kelly, their daughter, Allison, and new baby Zoe.

He hesitated to pick up the ringing phone. However, duty overcame reluctance. He took a deep breath and lifted the receiver. "Captain Anderson. How may I help you?"

"Afternoon, John, Curtis Oliver, here. Have some hot news. Got a call a couple of hours ago from a state trooper near Bastrop. Seems like some construction folks pulled a red car out of a stock pond on Bentsen Russell's old ranch. It was beat up pretty bad. Think you ought to come up and take a look see."

He gazed up at the ceiling and then out the window

at the traffic. "Red, huh? Same color off the rocks and the kid in that hit-and-run up on Mount Bonnell. Hmm."

"Yep."

"They impounding in Austin?"

"Reckon so."

"Then I'll see it in the morning. Thanks for the heads-up, Curtis."

Anderson picked up his briefcase and closed the door behind him. He smiled and pushed all thoughts out of his mind except those of Kelly and his girls. He often remembered the words she uttered the first evening they met.

"All work and no play makes John a dull boy."

JULIAN STUART HABER

also writes non-fiction.
Available at bookstores everywhere
or order personalized, autographed copies
at julianhaber@aol.com

ADHD The Great Misdiagnosis
Revised Edition, ISBN 1-58979-047-2
Taylor / Roman and Littlefield

This comprehensive review of the increasing frequency with which children are diagnosed with ADHD and the treatments available to those who actually have ADHD is invaluable to doctors and parents alike. Among other pertinent information, it includes how to deal with complicated legal issues in schools, teenagers with ADHD, and other conditions that complicate the disorder.

Other great stories from
Longhorn Creek Press

CHUTE #3
by Mackey Murdock
Mainstream fiction
ISBN 0-9714358-1-2

Go beyond the gates of big-time rodeo and straight into the hearts and lives of the remarkable characters who bring *Chute #3* to life. The emotions and memories this story evokes wrap the reader like an old quilt. You'll laugh. You'll cry. And you'll love Murdock's Texas Panhandle hero, Guthrie Sawyer!

Available at bookstores everywhere.
Order personalized, autographed copies from
www.LonghornCreekPress.com

THE PRICE PAID
by Ron & Caryl McAdoo
ISBN 0-9714358-7-1

Based on the true life experience of a WWII hellcat fighter pilot, this fictionalized account takes the reader along when his fuel line gets shot and he's forced to set down in the Pacific. A rescue plane comes, but then it has trouble taking off again. We all know the war's outcome, but this man's journey gives new insight into *The Price Paid*.

Available at libraries and bookstores everywhere.
Order personalized, autographed copies from
www.LonghornCreekPress.com

And Longhorn Creek Press is proud to share
these quality chapter books
for the younger blessings in your life.

THE ADVENTURES OF SERGEANT SOCKS
Book one THE JOURNEY HOME
by Grami & O'Pa McAdoo
Illustrated chapter book
ISBN 0-9714358-3-9

This heartwarming story of an orphan colt carried away from his newfound home by torrential floods well earns its many accolades. With the help of a few odd characters along his way, and remembering life lessons Uncle Dan taught him, Sarge determines to find his way back to his herd and the people who love him. Come along with the little colt on *The Journey Home*!

Available at all major booksellers and at
www.SergeantSocks.com.

THE ADVENTURES OF SERGEANT SOCKS
Book two THE BRAVEST HEART
by Grami & O'Pa McAdoo
Illustrated chapter book
ISBN 0-9714358-5-5

In this exciting adventure, the beloved orphan colt is waiting in the trailer with Uncle Dan when the whole rig is stolen! What the thief doesn't know is that two of the boss' grandsons are hiding in the tack compartment. Now the horses have to save the boys, and the boys have to save the horses. Besides bad men, Sarge faces a forest fire and a mountain lion. And he befriends a no-name filly who declares to all that he has *The Bravest Heart*!

Available at all major booksellers and at
www.SergeantSocks.com.

THE CHILDREN UNDER THE PLAYHOUSE
by Tricia Allen
ISBN 0-9714358-4-7

Depression-era orphans dodge adoption and hop a freight to Texas to find their actor uncle and be a real family again. Along the way, thirteen-year-old Gino, his sister Allie and his best friend Marcus encounter a bag of loot and a mysterious tycoon and his bloodthirsty henchman, but troubles worsen in Weathervane, Texas. Uncle Angelo's playhouse is boarded up and inhabited by an eccentric who wants him in jail. Gino tries to clear Angelo's name and winds up facing robbery charges and a frightening confrontation with the real bandits.

THE LEGEND OF RED LEAF
by Don Watson
ISBN 0-9714358-6-3

A Cheyenne girl is stolen and carried far away by the hostile Crow. When opportunity presents itself, she escapes and turns back. With the help of a lone wolf, Red Leaf begins her long and lonely journey home. Though suspicious of all white men, she comes to share a mutual trust with a mountain man who helps her and is helped by her. This engaging Old West historical captures hearts of young and old alike.

Coming early 2005

SIMMERING SECRETS OF WEEPING MARY
A Deuteronomy Devilrow Mystery
by Merry Hassle Frels
ISBN 0-9714358-9-8

Deuteronomy returns home for a family funeral, and the fun begins! Investigative skills acquired while staying with Miz Zan, a Ft. Worth police detective, coupled with Duty's natural curiosity and rural cunning, cause her to suspect favorite Cousin 'Miah was murdered — and she sets out to solve the crime in this charming new series.

Coming early 2005

AMAZING GRACI & THE RIVER BOTTOM GOATS
by Grami & O'Pa McAdoo
Illustrated Chapter book

This third delightful River Bottom Ranch Story introduces a newcomer to the ranch who comes to guard the herd of dwarf goats. The gentle Great Pyrenees not only has to deal with a jealous buck and a pack of wild dogs, but must earn the respect of the standoffish does for their own good. Graci discovers that she loves the kids in the herd most of all.

Coming May 2005

THE ADVENTURES OF SERGEANT SOCKS
Book three STRAIGHT AND TRUE
by Grami & O'Pa McAdoo
Illustrated chapter book

The boss ships Uncle Dan off, and Sarge gets an attitude. He doesn't understand that his folks think he's really fast and want to see if he can race, so he thwarts them at every turn. His antics get him noticed by a wealthy man who offers to buy him. Will the boss sell the beloved colt to save the ranch? Will Sarge be sorry he spouted off that not a cowboy alive could ride him? And, most of all, when the boss takes him to the track, will he run fast, *Straight And True*?

Coming Fall 2005

Watch for more details by visiting
www.SergeantSocks.com